WHAT MUSIC THEY MAKE/ THE CAPE

M. J. REISEN

authorHOUSE®

AuthorHouse™
1663 Liberty Drive
Bloomington, IN 47403
www.authorhouse.com
Phone: 1 (800) 839-8640

Published by AuthorHouse 10/04/2016

ISBN: 978-1-5246-4050-7 (sc)
ISBN: 978-1-5246-4051-4 (hc)
ISBN: 978-1-5246-4049-1 (e)

Library of Congress Control Number: 2016915580

Print information available on the last page.

WHAT MUSIC THEY MAKE

E verything a sheet of blue-white. While her eyes readjust, she counts under her breath, "One... two... three.. four..."

Then, from what seems like far away, there is a sound like rocks clattering down a mountainside, then-

BOOM!

The thunder grumbles as it slides away to the east after the initial discharge. A reedy voice pops up behind her: "'Bout four mahls away...", Corky Polouse slurs.

A whisper comes up from near her right shoulder, "The glass didn't even shake that time."

Evangeline turns and her eyes come to the level of the uneven part in Lula Mae's hair. With an exasperated, but tender sigh she realigns the thin, lank, brown strands with the grimy green ribbon in the small child's hair.

Not much more than a child herself, Evangeline has taken on the roles of mother, mentor and bodyguard to the waif. With Lula Mae's long-suffering mother gone and her father too saturated with shine to care, the pair gravitated to each other through the shared experience of abandonment and loss. All through the semi-regular grooming ritual, Lula Mae keeps her palm-pressed fixation on the window.

Another veined strobe of electricity streaks the sky. Two seconds later: BOOM!

Lula Mae yelps and jumps back from the window.

"Two mahls...", Corky drawled as he takes another pull on the jug that rests on the small table commandeered between himself and Wallace Burson.

"Eva!" Lula Mae grabs Evangeline's hand and places it over her heart. Evangeline feels the little muscle marching double-time as Lula Mae tries to suppress a smile of tremulous delight.

"Why you fussin' wid dat scarecrow? Ain't nobody gonna notice. Least of all her," Corky chuckles as he continues to lubricate his humor from the jug. Evangeline carefully inspects her hairdressing handiwork and tosses out carelessly: "You just say stupid stuff like that so I'll even look at you, PUH-LOUSE!"

Corky lunges out of his chair: "That's PUH-LOOSE, you ingnernt-"until he is interrupted by a stream of arcing tobacco juice that lashes across his face. "Hey-" Corky may not have a friend in the world, but that doesn't mean he is ever alone.

Wiping the spume away with his sleeve, he turns his hatchet face, contorted with consternation to the stolid figure that sat creaking in the rocking chair across from him. He is met with a twisted, amused grin. Where Corky's face is convex, with his domed skull, prominent nose and jutting chin, Wallace Burson's appearance is a yang to Corky's yin. A beetling brow, small deep-set eyes and a flattened nose and a bull dog jawline.

"Watch yo' manners 'round the flower of our Southern Womanhood. They may not be the rarest blooms, but that don't mean they should be shown such disrespect." Wallace could always be expected to weigh into any controversy, especially if he could equally denigrate everyone involved.

"Besides, she's got more learnin' than you got in yer whole family tree." And with that he lets fly with another jet of chaw, which pings accommodatingly in the spittoon. Then he closes his eyes, leans back in the chair, fingers laced behind his head. Corky shuffles his feet diffidently and settles back in his chair muttering under his breath just loud enough to be heard, but not readily understood.

Evangeline frowns and tries to concentrate harder on the task at hand. As her fingers weave their way through the lank tresses, her mind's eye calls up an image of Lula Mae from just a year earlier: attenuated shoulder blades – a baby bird fallen from the nest – as she lay prostrate in the mud, surrounded by a scrum of brats, taunting her outside of Granny Grace's dilapidated shack.

Something burst, hot and bitter in Evangeline's throat that day as she beheld this all too typical and unjust abasement of the meek. Before she knew it she had hurled herself into the puerile pack and weeping and yelling and pulling them each ten different ways from Sunday, scattered their erstwhile inquisition to the winds. As she stood there sobbing, her chest heaving with the effort and the emotion, she watched as the elfin creature merely picked herself up, make a brief swipe at brushing herself off and then trudge about the area, her eyes sweeping the ground. After a few seconds she pounced on a small pouch with a long drawstring that lay at the foot of a stunted oak tree.

Evangeline finishes with the hairdressing and scowls at the ill-fitting, faded smock on her small charge's spindly frame. Corky's taunts bit deeper than she would ever let on, for she did feel a deep shame and regret that her daily efforts would probably never improve Lula Mae's fortunes. She might be able to find her something to wear that was not so dingy, but because of what Lula Mae said her mama called her 'scolsis' it was difficult for anything to hang just right on her gaunt physique.

As she plucks fecklessly at Lula Mae's threadbare frock, her mind takes her back once again to realizing the enormity of what she had done. Having rescued her from exclusion and censure, Evangeline knew then and there that she had become responsible for this little, seemingly fragile, life. Sizing up the too large ears and feet, the too long neck, Evangeline knew that this child's plight was all too common around this sodden little isthmus in Clarke county. Lethe was just one of those ramshackle little hamlets on the delta that one might pass by wondering how on earth it's inhabitants could possibly eke out a living on such a sodden spit of clay.

The district had seen long years in reaping an all too commonplace story like Lula Mae's: her pappy was serving fourteen years in Wetumpka State Penitentiary for the manslaughter of her abused mother. The loss of her own parents in the 1912 influenza epidemic happened when Evangeline was not much more than an infant, so the bond was obscure, but it's lack indelible.

So, after having performed the rescue portion of her new mission, in imitation of the only responsible adult she knew-she thought of how her Uncle Thad always fussed over scrapes and cuts, instilling in her his own apprehensions of the inherent dangers of life lived on a tenuous margin where liquid was ascendent-she reached out and slipped her own slight arm over Lula Mae's delicate shoulders, patting gently and murmuring, "It's all right, it's gonna be all right...." as she surreptitiously scanned for injuries.

Her eye dropped to the soiled, but colorful little bag clutched in the raw-boned fingers. "What's that?", she rasped out. Lula Mae regarded the small sack as she rolled it between her fingers, "Granny Grace said it would keep me from harm, if I always kep' it."

"Didn't seem all the effective today", Evangeline retorted as she reached for the grubby talisman. Lula Mae intercepted Evangeline's hand with her own and placed it over her heart. Looking straight up into the older girl's eyes, she smiled, "It brought you." Evangeline felt her chest expand as if the very marrow of her essence was suffused with a lightness she had never known was possible or allowed.

"Sun's already down. Never seen clouds that black before," he says as he cranes his neck to peer out. Evangeline's portly uncle Thad hovered over the girls as he joined them at the window. His voice snaps her back to the present just as another flare of lightning blanches the gray-black world outside and heavy drops begin to spatter the already dank main street.

One... two....

Ba-ba-ba BOOM!

The whole building seems to lurch on it's foundation as the storm really puts it's foot down. Articles on the shelves that line the two sides of the store that stretch away from the entrance, rattle and clink. Lula Mae yelps and jumps back from the window. A cascade of rainwater lashes the windows, the wind moans and howls.

"Two mahls...", Corky drawls.

"Evangeline!" Lula Mae grabs Evangeline's hand and places it over her own heart. Evangeline feels the little muscle march double time as Lula Mae tries to suppress a smile of tremulous delight.

"Better to be getting' wet in here, than out there",Corky mutters as he grabs the jug, leans back, and drapes one arm over the back of his chair.

"Might not be that way for long. Evangeline, your assistance, please." Thad waddles towards the back room to fetch more containers to catch the rainwater that has started to plink and plunk around the store. Thadeus Walcott's Various and Sundry Dry Goods was a bit of a mouthful for the locals, so it became more popularly known as the 'V'n'S'; the most moist dry goods store in five counties.

Evangeline was about to comply to her uncle's request when she feels Lula Mae's heart skip a beat. Turning her gaze to the ashy face before her, Evangeline then follows Lula Mae's wide-eyed stare out the window. The wind has picked up and is driving the rain in tortured, rippling sheets. A dark bulk starts to coalesce out of the downpour. Slowly, it bumps along the always rutted thoroughfare, it's headlamps winking with each jostle like the eyes of a cat.

Now it is Evangeline's turn to press up against the window. A large, black hearse is lumbering ominously through the deluge like a mobile mausoleum. Since no one in this village rated a hearse, let alone a motorized one, Evangeline could only feel instinctively what the vehicle was for. Lula Mae's instincts seemed to have been aroused as well, because Evangeline feels a tugging at her waist. Lula Mae's elfin face, always rather wan, has taken on a waxy sheen causing her dark brows and almond shaped eyes to stand out in anxious relief. Never taking her eyes from the vehicle outside, she is slowly backing away from the window.

"Eva, Lula Mae, your assistance, please," Thad comes bustling out of the back with a clanging load of pots and pans. "Ya'll mind yo', mama, now." 'Show some respec' fer yer elders", comes the sniggering duet from the able-bodied males lounging in chairs by the pot-bellied stove. "Come on", Evangeline said as she takes Lula Mae's hand and marches quickly, eyes averted from the peanut gallery to where her uncle stands.

She takes two receptacles from her uncle and seeing that Lula Mae still seems distant and distracted, turns to see the macabre vehicle pass slowly by the storefront again. She pushes a dented pot into Lula Mae's hands and then steers her behind the counter on the east side of the store. Thad is now strategically placing oil lamps about the space as the electric current starts to show compromise with the lights dimming and flickering.

Just as Evangeline places her third vessel, the jangling bell over the front door peals and the wind flurries in on wailing tendrils before the door closes with a bang. Deliberate footsteps clomp on the wood plank floor and everyone turns towards the entrance to see standing under the Nehi Soda sign:

A tall figure in a long, dark, double breasted coat that reaches down to the tops of his wet boots. Hands shoved in his pockets, collar turned up, his face obscured by a dark gray pork pie hat with a black ribbon. To store's occupants he appears as impassive as a cigar store Indian.

His head slowly swivels to take in the entire store. He comes to a stop when he sees Lula Mae. Evangeline turns to find the young girl's gaze solemnly locked to the stranger's. She is about to move to Lula Mae's side when the newcomer turns and speaks to her uncle who stands by the storeroom door, "Good evening. Forgive the intrusion, but would ya'll be kind enough to direct a humble visitor the way to the Red Tide?"

His smile gleams eerily from the shadow formed by his hat brim and the harsh light from the one overhead electric light still burning – a bare bulb, swaying slightly and now flickering ominously in the deep gloom. The stranger doffs his hat. His hair appears as short, packed tight, glistening waves that rumple across his skull like freshly furrowed rows in bottom land. As the light strikes the tall man's eyes, they flare briefly with an amber hue.

"My apologies, gentlemen – and ladies. The weather is no excuse to forget my manners. I am Hawkshaw, at your service, I'm sure. We're strangers to hereabouts and would be much obliged for your gracious assistance." One rocking chair groans as it's load rolls off of it's seat. Wallace weaves slightly as he crosses to the front window and leans heavily on the frame, looking out.

Holding his hat in front of him, the new arrival continues to regard them calmly as the wind rattles the windows. Thad adjusts his glasses, sways slightly, then hesitantly shuffles forward as if his body was reluctant to follow his head, "Would you care for something hot to drink? We have some coffee if you care to-"

Hawkshaw waves him off, gently, "No, than you kindly, coffee isn't something that I-"

"Or another warm beverage?" Thad scrapes to a halt in front of the pot-bellied stove, the yellow-white light and heat wavering from it's seams make ripples through the murk. Combined with the light thrown from the rain drenched windows, the interior of the store seems submerged. Time and tide have slowed into an eddy. Thad starts to reach for the coffee pot on the top when-

"That your boat out there, Mr Ferryman?" Wallace calls from the window. Corky rises unsteadily from his chair and crosses to the window for a glimpse.

"Sayers & Scovill, nineteen-nineteen, seventy horsepower, six cylinders", Hawkshaw rattles off easily. "Got her second hand."

"No backseat driver's, I guess." Corky hiccups.

"You'd be surprised," Hawkshaw says.

Wallace turns from the window and looks him up and down, "This is a pretty tight-knit community. Nothing transpires around here without my notice. What's under the tarp? Another coffin?" Corky hiccups. Only then does it register with the others that there is another bulk lashed to a rack on top of the already imposing vehicle.

"Made a few adjustments, myself", Hawkshaw shrugs diffidently. "Besides, they kind of came with the deal. We're the evenings entertainment, a trio of roving minstrels is all. Just asking for some of that hospitality the South is so famous for and we'll be on our way."

Thad, still gawking at the stranger pours himself a small amount of coffee and shuffles forward abstractedly, "I don't know why, but I – have you ever passed this way before? And are you sure you wouldn't care for something hot-"

Hawkshaw demurs, "No, thank you kindly. If you'll just point me-"

"On a night like this, a man could use something a little stronger," Wallace says as he boots Corky in the rear, "Don't just stand there. Get our guest a real drink."

Corky stumbles to the table and upsets the spittoon much to Thad's dismay. Evangeline starts to laugh, but stifles it as she sees Lula Mae's impassive stare. Hawkshaw and Wallace are so focused on one another that they barely register the occurrence.

Hawkshaw, "It was my understanding that ya'll was *for* prohibition."

Wallace freezes. Then, turns slowly and squints at him, "And to whom would you be referring?" Evangeline notices the change in Wallace's diction and bearing since the arrival of the visitor.

"The South has it's own peculiar institutions," comes the cool rejoinder.

"A proud and time honored one being…. Moonshine?" Wallace leans heavily on the last syllable.

"Absolutely. Never afraid of a little white lightning," the response is calm, but the tone flattens out.

The two tall men seem to be engaged in a stare down. Thad rattles a spoon nervously in his cup, Corky has stopped sopping up his mess to watch. Evangeline can feel the air thicken and charge as if the tempest outside had seeped into the store. She looks to Lula Mae. Her eyes are fixed in the mid-distance and she is making subtle rocking and swaying motions as if dancing to some music only she can hear.

Wallace smiles and unexpectedly breaks the stalemate and crosses to the jug, "Well, tonight must be your lucky night because, you're right. Wardin' off any potential maladies brought on by foul weather is always a concern of this community." He hoists the jug onto his arm and takes a slug. Then he steps up to Hawkshaw as he slings it around and holds it out in front of him. Thad stops stirring, and Lula Mae ceases her gyrations.

"Medicinal purposes only, eh?" The taciturn musician never takes his eyes from Wallace's face.

"Something like that", Wallace chuckles.

"In that case-" Hawkshaw reaches out quickly with both hands and takes the jug from Wallace's grasp, wipes the spout, hoists it on his own arm, drinks and has it back in front of Wallace before he can even withdraw his hand. Evangeline grimaces and places her hand over her ears as she feels as if the atmospheric pressure in the room was increasing and beginning to take a toll on her middle ear.

"Sweep it clean, ain't gonna tarry here, Sweep it clean, ain't gonna tarry here...."

Five pairs of eyes swivel to the tiniest frame in the room. Lula Mae has now added singing to her bobbing and weaving with a whispering lilt. Evangeline drops her hands from her head and scurries over to the twisting tot and embraces her in an attempt to quell her stirring.

Corky, "There they go again. I swear, those two spastics ain't right no how."

Wallace barks, "Ha!" Eyes wide, but his face otherwise implacable, Wallace accepts the jug and swings it back over his shoulder as he crosses to the table and plunks it down, "Keeping comfortable in inhospitable weather is one peculiar institution around here. In Winter it's jug season, in Summer it's jar season."

"Ooh Lordy, ain't gonna tarry here, 'Cause he's diggin' down in the grave, ain't gonna tarry here…." The last electric light flickers out and only the lantern light now gives witness to the chinks and fissures in the store now streaming due to the squall outside now pummeling and buffeting every surface. Even the ox yoke and horse collars hanging from the ceiling are starting to channel water.

Hawkshaw, "These are some rare orchids you have here." He crosses over to the girls and kneels so that he is level with them. Lula Mae is now placid. Evangeline still embraces her from behind and clasps her tighter to her thin bosom.

"Like the Ghost Orchid, flourishing deep in the bayou where the darker elements of nature hold sway. Not only beyond man's reach, but also beyond his grasp." And with that Hawkshaw reaches out and gently cradles Evangeline's chin in his hand for an instant. A breathless moment passes between them.

Again the air seems to crackle with potential violence as Wallace's jaw muscles squirm with anger. His face is brutally underlit by the lantern throw. Then Thad lurches forward, "Just keep goin' the way you were headin' th' first time." He crosses to the window and gestures shakily with his free hand. Then it returns to reinforce his jittery hold on the cup. "'Bout a quarter mile down the road, you'll see it branch off to the left. Y-You can't miss it."

By this time Hawkshaw has straightened up and with a wink to the upturned visage of Lula Mae he crosses towards the front door. Before he has gone four steps the tempest outside seems to flutter and wane. By the time he places his hand on the door handle the only water coming down is sluicing from roof tops and eaves, no longer from the tortured sky. The receptacles in the store now only register desultory drips.

"Well, if that don't beat all…." Corky scratches his head.

Hawkshaw stops with his hand on the door handle. Tips his hat and says, "Be seeing you." And with that he opens the door and steps out into the becalmed, vaporous evening air. With his exit, the store's inhabitants seem to be as relieved of as much pressure as the local climate. It is only then that Evangeline looks to assess Lula Mae's condition. But, the fragile figure has vanished, leaving Evangeline puzzled and mortified at her inattention. Her eyes sweep the store with a growing sense of dread: she is nowhere in sight and Evangeline has no memory of releasing her.

Still under the influence of the alcohol and the mood from the recent atmosphere, Corky absently reaches for the jug as he weaves towards the table. As he retrieves it, he lifts it to his lips. Wallace strides over and dashes the jug out of Corky's hand. "What the hell-" Corky yelps.

Wallace glares at him, "What do ya think yer doin'? You know where that's been."

Evangeline doesn't stay to hear the rest. She bolts for the rear of the store and scans the storeroom and the sleeping areas with increasing alarm. No sign of her little charge.

Her heart quaking, she scampers out of the back door. Craning her head in all directions she works he way to the storefront where she sees: Lula Mae, running her hands over the base of the carved columns as she works her way along the street side of the ghoulish vehicle. She would love to feel the carved sconces and curtains, but she is too small to reach them easily.

Evangeline shivers as much from the sight of the macabre wagon as from the chill in the air that lingers from the front that has just passed through. Never fond of the dark, she nevertheless creeps closer to the vehicle, mud sucking at her feet, cold and clinging. Her attention is drawn to the white carved urn in window and then to the coffin encased behind it. With a shudder she turns away to find: Lula Mae has disappeared again.

Evangeline starts to slog her way towards the other end of the vehicle when a low chuckle emanates from behind her, "Well, ain't you just a sight for sore eyes."

She gasps and turns to see two red-rimmed eyes glittering at her from inside the passenger side of the hearse. The face looms closer to the door. The eyes barely clear the bottom of the window frame and the head seems a little over-large. "But, I don't think it's me you was lookin' for." The head nods and Evangeline turns to see Lula Mae picking her way across the street. Evangeline lowers her head and strides as quickly after her as the condition of the street will permit.

A slender figure with a small, bespectacled head topped by a straw skimmer steps from around the front of the hearse. He turns the collar of his trench coat up and adjusts his dark glasses as his gaze moves from

Evangeline to a thin, dirty-blond girl whose index finger traces back and forth across her lower lip as she stares at the ornate vehicle. He lifts his hat in greeting and smiles. The girl freezes. Then, as she is about to step forward, an arm bangs out of the ragged screen door and yanks her back inside. The figure by the hearse smirks as the tattered window shades also snap down on the weathered house front. He lets his gaze drift across the ramshackle storefronts, leaning to and fro, staggered like broken teeth in a stumble bum's mouth.

Hawkshaw exits from the store and steps out from the sodden wooden planks in front of the store to the even sloppier street and joins the other stranger. They stand in their long, dark coats and watch as the two young girls slip away down the street. They share a small smile, then Hawkshaw's partner opens the driver side door for him. He tips his hat and climbs in behind the wheel. The engine rumbles to life as the other band member opens the passenger side door and nods for the other occupant to make room, then slides in and slams the door closed behind him. The somber conveyance lurches into motion and slowly sloshes down the street.

E vangeline wobbles like a new-born fawn in trying to keep to the less sodden portions of the landscape. Having bolted out of the store without a thought to the current climate, her shivering with the damp night air makes for slow and treacherous footing as she treads tremulously past the skeletal piles of crab and crayfish traps near the quay at the edge of the town.

Even in this dim light, Evangeline knows the intended destination. And it only serves to increase her quaking anxiety. She tiptoes up to the edge of a small, familiar clearing. Peering though a small stand of scrub oak, she squints at an asymmetrical hovel, all but unrecognizable as a dwelling except for the weathered portal in front, a dimly lit porthole on the side and the straggling smoke that issues from a ramshackle chimney. Crickets trill and other creatures cloaked in the dark chant and sing all around her. The passing storm has christened the night with an invigorated flood of fauna.

Evangeline chatters with chill and fright as she makes her way carefully, but quickly to the door. She raps at the door and hugs herself, chafing her thin upper arms. From inside, the sound of a bolt being shot and then a shriek of wood as the door is wrenched open to reveal:

Six feet tall, barefooted, gray-green eyes and an auburn birth-mark streak in her hair, Granny Grace's granddaughter Chessie towered over most folks in the area in stature and reputation. She stares stolidly at the little blond girl before her. Then steps aside and holds the door open. Evangeline nods timorously and darts past her into the dim interior.

Corky always referred to Chessie as 'that High-yeller gal', though never in her presence. Evangeline and Lula Mae first encountered Chessie on one of their explorations around the delta. She was naked except for a cottonmouth snake, writhing across her shoulders. Mottled, dark with a banded head it was well over four feet long. Both the reptile and her current human trellis seemed quite unmoved at being discovered in this state. Indeed, it wasn't until the snake hissed in warning that Evangeline realized that her mouth was similarly agape.

Lula Mae, however had no trouble breaking the ice. She broke out into a commodious grin and waving one hand over her head, bellowed," Hi, yeller gal!" Even the waves seemed to hold their breath as the giantess stared at the tot oscillating at the water's edge. Then she let slip the serpent into the tide and stalked towards the shore as the serpent headed for deeper water. She splashed up to the tiny child and looked down on her. Lula Mae stared back in wide-eyed anticipation.

Then, Chessie scooped Lula Mae up in a robust arm and set her on her prodigious hip. With a nod of her head she indicated Evangeline to follow them and she strode away to a nearby bush draped with a crimson colored bolt of fabric. With her free hand, Chessie snatched it off of the shrub and loosely draped it around her and the little girl as they continued on to Granny Grace's. Evangeline thought it made the giantess appear more ancient, even Biblical.

These memories are what Evangeline conjured up as she made her way to the heart of the tumble down abode: the constantly stoked hearth. In order to reach it, however called for a circuit through a labyrinth of herbs, plants, animals, jars of specimens, concoctions and potions. Many of which Evangeline couldn't bring herself to look at. People came from all over, black and white to Granny Grace. Sometimes first, sometimes as a last resort, but they always came.

As she reaches the threshold of the hearth's glow she spies Lula Mae sitting in a small, rough hewn rocking chair by the hearth. Wrapped in a shawl, sipping something from a cup, her bare feet waving in the air. Her shoes and stockings are draped near the hearth. She smiles happily and non-nonchalantly at Evangeline. Then a coarse, grumbling voice rasps out from behind Evangeline causing her to flinch: "Lula Mae felt th' need to inform us o' strangers in town."

Granny Grace rocks her hips slowly past Evangeline and crosses to another chair by the fireplace. This one is padded and deeply ingrained with use. She pats the back of it as she turns to Evangeline, "Here. Take yo' wet things off." Evangeline walks meekly over and sits. As she starts to remove her shoes, Granny, already bowed with age reaches down and takes over, helping to remove both shoes and soiled stockings.

Granny was said to be in her 90's. But, most of the longest time inhabitants have seemed to think that for years, so in essence no one really knew her age. Her voice had the indiscriminate buzz that comes with the slack of age and lack of tooth, but most of what she emitted was intelligible once one was acclimated to the sound.

"Here", she said to no one in particular as she holds out the shoes and stockings. Then, a figure looms into the penumbra of light cast by the fire and takes the objects from her narrow, wavering hand. Evangeline looks up to see Chessie, clad in a red skirt with a white blouse. She exchanges Evangeline's garments for a cup and saucer which she hands in turn to Granny Grace. The old woman offers the drink to the young girl, her gaunt hand causing the cracked china to chatter together.

Evangeline gratefully takes the proffered beverage and takes a tiny, testing sip. The tea is quite hot and she winces with the scalding of her lips and tongue. But, she was grateful for the warmth and it was a tea she was familiar with. In it's un-brewed state, it's aroma was redolent of nothing so much as an un-mucked stable but, once steeped offers a slightly gritty, but warm, earthy taste that is quite appealing while hot.

Granny stands before the two girls and looks from one to the other, "Coulda saved you's a trip. I'm not surprised, I could tell by th' weather. No ordinary storm. No, siree. And Miss Evangeline afraid of the dark."

She cackles lightly and turns away and scuffles away towards the dark as Chessie stands impassively looking on as is her wont. Even though most of her folk had fled to seek prosperity in practically every direction they could from Lethe, Granny stayed. It was not a unique story in this town. Nor for many around the county and state. Many families had become friable in order to survive and such rampant dislocation and relocation was a great source of fission and friction everywhere.

Chessie moves a chair into the warm circle and Granny totters over to it and gradually lowers herself into it. Once there, she leans back with a sigh and absently picks at the hairs on her chin as she murmurs,""Yep. Gettin' ta be time for a new Exodus. A new Moses to lead to the Promised Land."

Chessie retires back into the dark recesses of the burrow with Evangeline's things. Evangeline looks over the rim of her cup at Lula Mae. "What did you tell them?" Lula Mae stares blankly, then shakes her head and shrugs.

Evangeline, "She and the tall black man, they was-"

Granny, "They took a shine to one another?"

Evangeline frowned in concentration, so she did not see the miniscule smile the old lady had pressed on her lips. "She was kinda like those people in church when just before they start fallin' over and the spirit flows through 'em and they start talkin' like-"

"Dark he was and golden eyed," Granny mutters to no one in particular. Evangeline looks sharply at Lula Mae who only shrugs again in return.

Chessie hovers into sight again, she is carrying a tea pot and she refreshes Lula Mae's drink. The flames flicker minute rainbows of color across the pale opalescent skin that asserts her mixed heritage. Then she hovers over Lula Mae and reaches down and gently strokes her hair. The spare child preens under the weighty hand and smiles up at the giantess. The smile is not returned. No one in the county had ever remembered her having done so at any time. But, that in no way mitigated what seemed to Evangeline an essentially beneficent nature. The mutual and tender orbit that the seemingly mismatched pair of Lula Mae and her made that seem obvious if nothing else.

"They was like you," Lula Mae says quietly. Chessie stops the caress and straightens up. "Are you gonna go with them when they go?" The tyke asks as she sips at her cup, her eyes large and appealing. Chessie looks at Granny who stares back. Then the old woman speaks as if to no one in particular: "Bank went under, farm went under, worked for the rail road cutting ties. Two dollars a day. Seven kids. Chessie's pa. Chessie's Ma took in sewing at nine."

Lula Mae looks to Chessie. Chessie looks from Granny to Lula Mae, then turns and saunters out of the circle of light. Lula Mae looks to Evangeline who can only shrug in return. Granny starts up again, "Winds of change. Time for young people to move on. Water doesn't stay in one place. Most of the world is water. Most of people is water. Why should they be any different?"

Granny falls silent and seems to chew over her last pronouncement. Evangeline thinks over the litany and feels compelled to make an observation, "That sounds like a lot of families. Colored and white 'round here." She keeps her head bowed and stares at her cooling tea cup. She learned early on that to bring the two races up in one conversation could have a deleterious effect on the reaction of adults.

Granny turns her head to the child and stares for a moment, then rocks herself up and out of the chair and crosses to the waif. Her shrunken stature almost brings her face to the level of Evangeline's.

"What falls from above falls on everyone's head. They is some who think just cuz they heads is covered, that the tide won't keep from risin' above their chin." She reaches down and gently fingers a few wisps of sallow hair on top of the imp's head, "You're young. You can learn to float. You got more time aheada you than you know."

Then she tosses another statement out, seemingly to the general air, "Make sure ya'll tell Red it's gonna be heaps o' customers tonight at the Tide."

She straightens up as much as she is able which adds perhaps three inches to her current height and hobbles her way deeper into the dark obscurity of her abode/apothecary. Just as she revolves out of the circle of light, Chessie appears," The band is supposed to be hot as they played around the country; Nawlins, KC."

Lula Mae leaps up from her chair, "Jus' like Joshua fit de battle of Jericho." She smiles and dances in circles, arms spread wide, eyes closed, head tilted back in reverie. She twirls to Evangeline and pulls her out of the chair, the pair titter and careen about. Until they almost collide with Granny as she appears once again at the edge of the firelight.

Granny draws herself up at that and fixes a critical eye on the girls, "Someone needs to read the Good Book mo' careful. First of all they was seven ram's horns, so Joshua wasn't the only one blowin'. An' after seven days of that it still takes Joshua orderin' his peoples to give their war cry that finally brought them walls a tumblin'."

She crosses to Lula Mae who has stopped her twirling and is now listening gravely, "It was the people. The power o' th' people what brought the city low. Stren'th in numbers." She caresses Lula Mae's head tenderly. The little child shivers as she looks into the old woman's eyes, but offers a tremulous smile at the tenderness of the caress.

Granny, "You best get Hercules ready. If'n you 'spect to be getting' these two back." She turns from the child to Chessie who once again hovers into the edge of the firelight. Lula Mae slides abruptly off of her chair and tugs at the hem of Granny's threadbare and eccentrically layered garments. The old woman turns as the youngster looks up at her with concern, "Can't we stay? Just a little longer?"

Evangeline now bolts off of her seat and sets her cup carefully down on the battered end table next to her, "We really should get goin', Lula Mae. Uncle'll be worried."

Lula Mae's chin drops to her chest in disappointment as she pouts softly,'I wanted to hear Granny tell us about the strange men."

Evangeline, "Lula Mae was doin' her 'trance dance' when the tall man was in the store."

Chessie and Granny share a conspiratorial glance. Granny sets her fists on her hips and tilts her chin in the air, "Their fate is they own concern."

Lula Mae fingers her tea cup in an agitated fashion and offers hopefully, "Can we get a reading before we go?" She finally looks up and extends the tea cup to Granny who merely purses her already corrugated lips and looks from one to the other. Then ignoring the offered cup, "You two have a chained destiny. Don't need nothing to tell me that."

The two tots beam at each other with barely suppressed glee. Granny continues in the same grave fashion, "That don't mean it's gonna be easy. You'll have to rely on that chain to pull each other up from time to time." The two little girls lean into one another and their fingers entwine.

"Ya'll need to remember one thing: that anything that don't keep you alive is too small for you. The world is a lot bigger than you can see now, "Granny reaches down and checks to see if Lula Mae has her gris-gris. She lifts the little satchel and shakes it gently in the little girl's face, "Take what you will from here. It's magic is carried over the air or in the water."

She replaces the talisman on the child's thin chest with a gentle pat and turns and heads for the cluttered and aromatic area of her hovel where she practices her apothecary, "Now, I'm gonna get your Unckle Thad's herbs together." She shoos the two young ladies towards their belongings, "Ya'll get ready now, yo' stuff should be dry enough." The girls look at each other, then scamper to the fireplace hearth and begin to fondle their articles of clothing and find them – yes, practically dry.

Granny, "Better get a move on if'n you gonna get this pair back where they belong, my chere."

Chessie, "I'll have Red pick me up after I drop them off."

Granny, "Don't forget to give him some money for gas. Your mama's letter arrived from Birmingham, we got the cash."

She looks back at the girls; Evangeline is seemingly in wonder at the parched nature of her shoes and socks and is still seated on the hearth. Lula Mae has finished dressing and stands behind the older girl, trying to work through the damp tangles of her thin blonde hair. The two women watch them:

Chessie, "What ain't you tellin' them?"

Granny, "I do what I can to saves people as much mis'ry as possible. Try to keep things in balance. Most we can hope for in this life." She finishes her collection of herbs and tonics and wraps them up in a bag for the girls.

Twenty six minutes later Chessie leads a charcoal colored mule with a white belly up through the main street of town. Lula Mae clings to the animal's mane while Evangeline is wrapped around her from behind. They are all engaged in song, the rhythm roughly corresponding to the mule's casual gait:

Sweep it clean
Ain't going to tarry here
Sweep it clean
Ain't going to tarry here
O-o-o Lordy
Ain't going to tarry here
'Cause he's digging down in the graveyard
Ain't going to tarry here

As intimidated as Evangeline and even Lula Mae could be around the mysterious lair of Granny Grace and her towering granddaughter (as she called her), they always felt more welcome and comfortable in the African-American community. They found their own race to be full of superstition and a general lack of trust in anyone even their own relatives. Although they witnessed some of the same behavior in the colored community, their marginal status as citizens helped to make them feel quite simpatico.

Also, they seemed a more cohesive and celebratory society. The girls loved the songs and patter that would punctuate even the most mundane, every day experiences. And the music. Since Chessie had begun work at the local roadhouse for the Negro population, they thrilled to stories of the musicians famous or infamous that would occasionally roll through. A few times, Chessie would get them to stop by Granny's as her reputation as a soothsayer and healer would sometimes precede her. They would spend rapturous hours, listening to tales of other times and places. And even be treated to a tune of two, if the occasion permitted.

It was Chessie's idea to strike up in song once she saw that Evangeline was reacting very nervously to the various nocturnal sounds of nature. With the mule's lead in one hand and an ancient lantern dimly flickering in the other, her low alto rumble gave an anchoring resonance to the treble pipes of the two girls and buoyed them up through the dark passage to home.

As they approach the 'V'n'S' Evangeline cranes her neck around Lula Mae to catch a view of the large storefront window,"Oh, good. They're gone."

"I thought you said they headed for the roadhouse," Chessie scowls.

"Oh, I meant Corky and Wallace," Evangeline responds as she settles back.

Chessie's response is a snort of derision. As she brings the animal to a halt in front of the store's steps, Thad emerges from the entrance, glowering. But, as Chessie lifts Lula Mae off of the mount, his expression softens and he rubs his hands together in a flustered fashion, "Well, well… thank you so much for returning these little fugitives…"

Chessie does not respond as she helps Evangeline down from the mule's back. Lula Mae climbs the steps and hugs one of Thad's thighs. One hand drops on her head and musses her hair but addresses Chessie, "How's your mama likin' life in the state capitol?"

Chessie, "Says she misses the honest red clay of home to the soot and grime of the city. Can't seem to get clean no matter how much water you use." She blows out the feeble flame in the lantern and uses the steps to mount the mule, "Well, I best be getting' back. They'll be comin' to pick me up soon."

Thad, "Oh, yes. The folk all have their antenna up." Evangeline sidles up to her uncle and he prods both girls, "Ya'll thank Chessie for looking after you and seeing you safely home." They comply with shy waves and murmured gratitude. As Chessie nods in acknowledgment and flicks the reins, the disparate trio watch Hercules and his Amazon trot into the shadows of the darkened main street.

3

'**R**ed' Mingus is short, stocky, with massive upper arms. His scarred lips pursed in doubt, he quickly wipes at them with an ever present handkerchief as if the gesture will relieve them of their tension. He eyes the rain water still dribbling from the eaves of the squat, former warehouse, then casts a dubious eye at the still leaden, but now seemingly depleted clouds overhead. The sudden torrent had him scurrying to mitigate heretofore latent leaks in the roof of his club. He knows he will have to leave soon to pick up his wait staff and anxiously scans the west for the arrival of the evening's entertainment.

He mutters to himself as he paces back and forth and is about to head back inside to wake his dilatory nephew to try and persuade him to take the car to pick up the two waitresses. It was hard to tell what the youngster's response would be. Being able to drive the car, a 1912 Colby with a well patched canopy and tires was no real pleasure in itself save for the motion and the relative autonomy and responsibility (an ethic he usually avoided with varying degrees of success). And Chessie being one of the passengers was sure to intimidate the boy. No, only the reedy allure of Ella Lee's figure and big brown eyes might motivate his sister's aimless son. He should be up by now any way. The sun was down.

As he turns one last time to appraise the sky, he catches a glint of light out of the corner of his eye. He drops his gaze to the horizon and straightens up to peer into the thickening darkness. Hands on hips, he raises himself up on his toes and cranes his head about. Then he sees it again, closer this time – two pale globes weaving and bobbing their way towards him. He rocks back on his heels as the grumble of the vehicle's engine is piggybacked to him in the cooling night air.

As the conveyance looms closer, the proprietor of the Red's Tide finds his mouth agape with perplexity as he recognizes the usual purpose of the unique transport. The lights snap off several yards before it rumbles to a stop. It stands quivering until the motor rattles to a halt. The ensuing silence presses down like increased atmosphere. The doors to the cab crack open simultaneously. Red eyes the driver critically as he steps out and fits a pork pie hat on his head with a deliberate motion and runs his finger around the front of the brim in a finishing gesture. He dips his hands into the pockets of his long overcoat and strides evenly towards the proprietor.

In the background, Red can see two figures clambering about the uncanny vehicle, divesting it of receptacles of various size and configuration. The driver walks up to and past the proprietor, so Red scoots to keep up with the tall stranger's long strides, "This storm may keep people away. But, we hear you blow your brass like Buddy Bolden at the Funky Butt, so maybe folks'll be curious enough to brave the weather."

As they reach the front door, Red slips ahead and holds it open for the band leader. The musician doffs is hat and steps into the small makeshift foyer. Red gestures for him to step into the next space and he does so to find-

A large open space with a fifteen foot ceiling. The room extends back about one hundred feet with a bar along the west wall about twenty feet in length. There are a pair of swinging doors at the far end of the bar in a jutting wall that leads to the kitchen. Just then the other band members come in, bearing as many instrument cases as their hands will hold.

The musician carrying the bass fiddle case sports an open collar shirt shirt and a straw boater with a grosgrain ribbon which he tips in greeting to Red. The drummer, dwarf-like in stature, but with long arms drops his load, and pulls his derby hat down over his face and nods towards the bar.

Hawkshaw follows his gaze. He purses his lips in concern and nods back at his band mate. He turns to Red, "Thank you for inviting us to your splendid edifice. May we make one request?"

Red hesitates slightly, then, "Sure, sure."

Hawkshaw, "Could you please see that the mirror behind the bar is completely draped? The reflective surface can make our little ensemble sound rather brittle."

Red looks at him quizzically for a moment, then turns to face the mirror. With fluted columns and scroll work of oak similar to that of the musician's vehicle, it runs almost the entire length of the bar.

He turns his gaze back to Hawkshaw and begins diffidently, "Well that piece is kinda special to my sister, see-"

He stops short as he looks up into the musician's face. Although the smile is mild enough, there is something in Hawkshaw's eyes that is so commanding the smile cannot reach it and Red cannot help but acquiesce to it, "Sure, sure. I'll get my sister's boy right on it."

Hawkshaw allows his grin to widen to his other features, "Thankee kindly." He strolls back towards the bandstand to join his partners.

Red shakes his head as if to clear it and in doing so recalls an issue he feels that needs to be breached," Heard it through the grapevine you made some acquaintances at the V'n'S."

Hawkshaw, "Can't hurt to advertise."

Red, "It can if you end up peddlin' your wares to the wrong customers. Around here it's better to know the lay of the land. Us colored folk got our own ways and means of getting' the word out that is a lot-"

"Safer?" Hawkshaw suggests as he removes his coat and hat.

"More…. exclusive," comes the diplomatically phrased reply.

"That doesn't sound like a very wise business practice. There's nothing to be ashamed of here." He opens his case and starts to assemble the horn inside.

Red, "Not ashamed. Just….careful."

Red runs his handkerchief over his closely cropped head," Listen, we all what's got to live here have a mind to keep on doin' so. Blood been shed over this land for over three hundred years and too much of it has been from folks like us. And we is owed something for that and we don't intend to lose any mo' of what we got."

Hawkshaw, "Which is precious little."

Red, "We get along during the day. What we do at night has always been our business."

Hawk, "It's not the nocturnal activities of the colored community that this town needs to concern itself with."

Red, "Which is what I been sayin'. Let's not give anyone any reason to-"

Chessie, "Ain't white folks business what a bunch of darkies do for kicks 'mongst themselves."

They turn to see her sling what looks to be a large and heavy laden purse onto the bar. She removes a clock from her purse and after scowling at the barkeep who has just finished cover the mirror with an old, tattered tarp now pulls out her own mirror which she places on the bar top, then pulls out a large comb and sets about arranging her long, curling tresses into a shorter and more manageable configuration.

Hawkshaw smiles at her, but addresses Red," A lot of things happen in the night that can't stand the light of day. Music isn't one of them." And with that he starts warming up his horn with soft 'bleeps' and 'blaps' that puff from the bell.

Red, "We been plannin' this night for a dog's age. But, that storm was like the plagues of Egypt. The land is crawlin' with snakes and toads swarmin' like kudzu and rats as big as cats up among the Spanish moss, people are sayin'." He shakes his head and mutters, "They's a bad moon risin'."

Hawkshaw, "You'd be surprised at the affect that music has on people." He turns away evoking strangled, muted tones as he flexes his emboucher. Red stands, mopping his brow, shaking his head when a rim shot startles him.

"You just met one of the original monologists, my man," Elvin offers as he slings down two heavy instrument cases with unconscious ease to the floor of the bandstand. "Ain't that right, 'T'?

The anxious proprietor plucks his sodden linen from one hand to the other as he traipses back towards the stand, his eyes still focused on Hawkshaw and muttering, "He don't give much away, do he?"

'T',"Solid, 'E'. The way I hear tell it is, he picked up with Kid Ory's band when they swung back from the West coast. Been ridin' the roadhouse circuit through the South since then. He hooked me up right outside Shreveport."

Elvin, "Sat in with the likes of King Oliver, Bessie Smith, Jelly Roll...."

Red continues to fret, oblivious of the impressive resume that is recited before him, "Blacks are scared. White's riled up...."

'T', "Don't you worry none about the bush apes 'round here. After tonight, they'll see things in a different light."

Red scowls and looks askance at T, "How you figure?"

'T" smiles enigmatically as he kneels on the stage with a hammer and nails, "It all starts with the music. You'll see." Elvin sees this and places his hands over his ears and heads for the exit, "I'll be outside." 'T' chuckles at his retreat and begins to anchor the bass drum to the planks of the bandstand, driving the nails in with three hard swings each. He looks up to see that Chessie is just finishing her grooming and leers at her, "Mm, mm, mm."

Red follows his gaze to the bar and back. Then he chuckles nervously at 'T', "We could have enough ruckus tonight without you starting anything."

"Don't you fret none, Pops. I is the soul of charm and discretion," he offers as he straightens up, dusts himself off and cocks his ever present bowler to a rakish angle. But, he doesn't get three steps before Hawkshaw appears and snags him by the shoulder, "You gotta learn to read the signs better, my young brother. She is in a league by herself." 'T' looks at the hand on his shoulder, then up into the band leader's face, then over to Chessie who has collected her things and is heading for the double doors of the kitchen.

Hawkshaw squeezes the drummer's shoulder for emphasis and 'T' turns his gaze back to Hawkshaw. He considers the advice, then nods slowly and retreats back to his drum kit. Hawkshaw turns to Red and continues his argument from earlier, "It would be a great disservice to yourself and your community to deprive it's citizens of a communal activity. What we can offer is more than just an evening's entertainment." He wets the mouthpiece, inserts it and eyes it before he raises it to his lips. "Music can make folks see their lives in a whole new light." He turns and moves slowly away, making small 'bleeps' and 'blats' with his horn as he begins to synch his body's rhythm to the instrument.

As he reaches the front doors, they swing open and he strides out into the open air. Elvin, stands one hand holding a door as Hawkshaw seems to sink into himself, then he raises up on his toes, his knees buckle and he leans back forming a sort of inverted 'S' shape. The clarion tone that blasts out shifts into an overtone that rings and reverberates through the crisp expurgated night. The lingering clouds seem to move slowly away south, back over the shimmering gulf waters.

Elvin smiles and wriggles a little finger around in one ear to help clear the piercing effect of the horn. 'T' stands in the doorway, doing a little Charleston step, his head nodding, chanting softly with glee to himself, "Oh, ashes to ashes and dust to dust, I said, ashes to ashes and dust to dust, if my blues don't get you, my jazzing must!"

Hawkshaw turns to him, "Now, "T', you know we don't use that word. It's social music." Then with a genial grin he turns to Red who stands in the open doorway his face slack with wary astonishment, "They'll come."

Lula Mae seemed delighted to be home and Evangeline was grateful and relieved. Dinner consisted of red beans and rice and collard greens. Thad even fried up a little bacon as an extra treat because of the weather and well, just because.

"Lula Mae, don't forget to brush your teeth and hair and say your prayers before you-" Thad comes to a puzzled halt as he rounds the corner into the girl's room. Before him, poised on her knees, her elbows resting on the bed, her hands palm-pressed together in devotion, head bowed, eyes closed is the object of his admonishments. Evangeline hears his exhortation trail off and steals up to his side, still brushing her teeth. She, too pauses in surprise at the marvel before her. Any other night while it might be possible to persuade the tot to brush her teeth by herself, she always insisted on having Evangeline brush her hair and cajole her to execute her prayers. It seemed a necessary ritual for the young girl's ease.

But, tonight, Evangeline and her uncle watch in wonder as the foundling finishes her whispered invocations with an emphatically whispered, "Amen!" Then she clambers under the coverlet and pulls the cover up to her chin and finally turns her gaze to the room's other occupants. Evangeline and Thad share a baffled glance as it was also unheard of Lula Mae to tuck herself in. Just as they were considering a consultation over these remarkable occurrences, the recumbent child pipes up, "Can we maybe have a bedtime story?" The two look back at her as she clutches her only doll to her breast, then to each other. Thad gently nudges Evangeline to her own little cot and pulls back the cover to help tuck her in, "What kind of story?"

Lula Mae barely pauses, "The one where all the animals was saved from the flood."

Evangeline had seen the kind of deprivations and degradations that the community of color was constantly subjected to and felt an empathetic kinship with them just as she had with Lula Mae. They were colorful, full of stories and song. And had a sense of caring community that she found rare in her own circle. So, they always tried to encourage similar customs in their own small sphere of influence.

"Which one?" comes Thad's mundane response as he seats himself on the edge of Evangeline's cot which creaks with the added burden. "The one where Gligamesh saves an immortal man and his family as well as the animals by building a big boat in Mesopotamia, or the one in India, where Vishnu tells the first man to build a boat for an upcoming flood, or when Prometheus told his son to build a vessel to save them from the wrath of Zeus' deluge?"

The girls exchange disconcerted glances, "Who, what, where….?"

"Did they have floods in all those different places?" Evangline finally asks.

"Well, the floods were supposed to be world wide, but people back then didn't really know just how big the world was." He replies, picking absently at the bed cover. "But, all these different places and people came up with pretty much the same story."

"Like Noah in the Bible," Lula Mae affirms.

"Yep," Thad says as he fusses with the cover around Evangeline's pillow. She looks up at him, "Why do you think they did that?"

Thad shrugs and finishes swaddling the tow-headed tot and and turns back, "I think they felt things were not going right, and that people were unhappy and wanted to start again, try something different."

"Did they save all the animals?" Lula Mae asks through an enormous yawn.

Thad smiles and assures her, "One of each." He turns to Evangline," Supposedly, Noah didn't sleep at all because he had to take care of all the animals and-"

He breaks off as a soft snuffling sound calls his attention back to the other child – Lula Mae snores lightly, clutching her doll to her chest outside the coverlet. He looks back to his niece, they share a smile. He kisses her quickly on the forehead and smooths her bangs as he rises from the jittery bunk, "Sweet dreams, Eva."

"'Night, uncle," she responds as she turns on her side and closes her eyes. Thad looks them over fondly for a moment, then retreats, pulling the curtain across the open doorway to their small inner sanctum of nocturnal speculations.

As Evangeline drifts towards sleep, she thinks back over the day. Her eyelids droop and flutter as she gazes at Lula Mae's face. Her dozing mind evokes a kaleidoscope of images from her first encounter with her small companion. The small tribe of unruly children who taunt her prone form swoop and screech, their voices becoming louder and distorted until they resembling nothing so much as a rabid pack of brute beasts.

Evangeline tries to make her way towards her friend, but seems to be hindered by an increase in the dream's gravity, her legs churn, but the only progress she seems to make in any direction is down. Down and down she goes until the dream slips away into darkness.

W allace Burson stands with hands on hips, a scowl creasing his
arcane features as he scans the scene before him. He claps his
hands over his face and holds them over his eyes to obviate the sight.
All around him swirls a maelstrom of sounds: the baying of hounds, the
whinnying of horses, the rumble and backfire of primitive combustion
engines. He wipes his hands angrily from his face and stalks towards the
front door of O'Leary's barn. He watches as jugs of corn liquor are passed
freely. Wallace strides up to the small knot of gatherers and snatches a jug
from Corky's hands. As he enters the building he can hear disgruntled
voices trailing behind him.

Corky, "Aw, c'mon, Wallace. You know the boys like to have a little
lubrication before-

"Reviewing policy", Wallace snaps as he crosses over to a makeshift
stand of hay bales and plywood on which a table and a small, scarred
schoolroom lectern sits on the table top. The small circle that follows him
groans collectively.

Corky, "We all thought prohibition was more of a guideline than a
rule. Damn, Wally you sound just like that nigg-."

Wallace slams the jug on a table at the end of the room with one hand,
then grabs Corky by the front of his robe with the other. All eyes turn to
him and the din of babbling, querulous voices trickles to a halt. Wallace
lets the silence deepen as he slowly sweeps the assemblage with a stern gaze.
Then he shoves Corky contemptuously away and smooths his own robes as
he takes up the prominent position behind the small podium.

Wallace, "Nine years ago, the South rose again in that phoenix of Dixie; Atlanta. And since that time, the sacred cause of 'One Hundred Percent Americanism' has blessed us with a fraternity of millions." He spreads his arms as of to present such a multitude to his own not insignificant gathering. He pauses for the enthusiastic response which does not disappoint as the gathering explodes in applause with shrill yips, yelps and yahoo's.

Wallace now gives a twisted grin of satisfaction as he recognizes faces from at least three other counties in the SRO crowd,"With our assembly tonight, we witness the proud heritage we bear with our fine array, our solemn rituals and our dedication to the purity of this great nation and to it's far thinking founders. And this Spring our influence was obviously felt when Washington finally started to realize that this proud and sacred land must no longer be influenced or infiltrated by those who do not share this great heritage of freedom and would threaten to defile it's consecrated destiny."

More whoops and yells and whistles, even louder and cacophonous than before rattle the rafters. Dust and hay particles flutter and eddy through the air like organic confetti.

Wallace continues, slowly building to an inexorable climax, "We don't take our orders from Washington!"

"No!" comes the reverberating choral response.

"We don't take our orders from Rome!"

"No!"

He raises his right hand as if in pledge, "And let the Pharaoh's of the old South beware. We take our calling from our native soil which has been irrigated with the blood from our veins for generations. Our strength is in numbers. In sworn brotherhood!" He throws out his arm, palm down, slicing the air before him.

His audience is now stamping it's feet and the cries have become more raucous and feral sounding.

Wallace leans on the table and waits out the clamor and as it abates, he drops his voice to an intimate level but heightens the urgency in his delivery, "A storm front is coming. Lightening strikes where it will and there's no reason it can't happen here. It will spread a wildfire to purify, to cauterize the wounds inflicted on this great country by those who would bastardize it, dilute it. Then a great flood of patriotism to sweep the land clean and revitalize it. Only in purity can there be harmony, peace and order!"

Thirty right arms snap out from thirty white clad chests, palms down, fingers extended and in unison they chant, "To relieve the injured and the oppressed. To shield the sanctity of the home!"

Wallace once again passes his gaze over his cohorts. Standing with their arms outstretched shoulder high in their robes, he suddenly felt as if he were leading a council of Roman Senators into battle. With a satisfied growl he utters, "Tonight, we ride." But, the vow is submerged under waves and waves of pent up resentment overly lubricated with alcohol, that crashes and roars like a hurricane from one end of the enclave to the other.

E vangeline awakes with a start. She is having a hard time catching her
breath. Then she realizes why – she is treading water. This sudden
revelation causes her to panic and she slips under the surface. She flails
herself back up to the surface, spluttering and gasping. As she struggles to
keep afloat, she corkscrews her body around in the chilled water.

Wherever she is, it is dark and there is no hint of a breeze. The only
illumination comes from her gyrations which sends yellow-green flames
licking across the surface of the drink until their phosphorescence fades
into the murky distance. She can discern no horizon. Just as this knowledge
induces another shock, she-

Wakes with a start. Her heart hammering in her small chest she finds
herself sitting up in her own bed, in her own room. Placing a hand over
her heart she make a conscious effort to slow it's rhythm and collect her
breathing. As the noises of her own alarmed body begin to wane in her
ears, another sound begins to register – music.

Just as in her dream, she finds herself twisting her body slowly to
locate the source of the sound, but it has faded. Was it even there? But,
in the process her gaze travels over Lula Mae's bed. At first, the sight of
the doll propped up by the scrunched up coverlet seems unremarkable.
Then, Evangeline sits up abruptly in bed. The music in her head stops. She
throws off the thin blanket covering her and leaps to Lula Mae's bedside.
After some trepidation she snatches the coverlet off of the bed, sending the
stacked pillows underneath and tattered doll to the floor.

Staring at the bed that is obviously bereft of her friend, Evangeline
feels an impulse welling up from deep inside of her. She is not sure how it

will manifest itself. Suddenly, she realizes that she has stopped breathing and spots appear before her eyes and she crumples onto the pile of pillows next to the doll that used to be hers.

Saturday night. The angry, scouring rain of dusk has polished the air, leaving a gleaming night sky. Wispy clouds drift over the full moon like a silk scarf trailing over the throat of a courtesan. There is a crisp coolness to the air left behind by the storm.

Hawkshaw sits at the house piano in his shirt sleeves-a battered but in tune 1907 Wellington upright, and noodles at the keyboard as the other band members hang loose on the bandstand, "The three hundred miles that separated the two of you would've taken eight days to cover on the road less than twenty years ago. Now it can be covered in a day."

The club staff all move at their own singular pace. Red, anxiously mopping his brow as he goes from person to person cajoling them each in an individual way. Except for Chessie who moves at her own regal pace and with whom Red respectfully consults when he approaches her at all. Ella keeps finding ways to hover around the bandstand despite the efforts and the obvious glowering censure from Red's barkeep nephew.

"Man has sought to expand his sway over the world by pushing against the darkness with his electric lights." He shakes his head. "Just like ya'll still need schoolin' on the gone by, you need to watch out for the modern, too. All this stuff I been talkin' about will come together like a web, a net. And it'll snag you unawares if you don't watch out."

Ella has lighted on the edge of the stage again. She and 'T' keep exchanging playful glances. The nephew also sidles up to the stage so that his leg bumps Ella with seeming inadvertence. Then something catches his eye-

Les Enfants du Noir is inscribed on the bass drum.

The barkeep tilts his head as he puzzles over it," Lez enfants doo no....ear....?"

Elvin, "It's French."

Red, "You mean like Cajun." He suddenly looms over Ella and his nephew. The girl cringes and slinks back to work under his dire scowl. Then he turns back to the musicians, "We is gettin' ready to open in a few minutes. I been so busy I ain't had a right chance to check the gate, yet. Ya'll ready?" He wads his handkerchief from hand to hand.

'T' spins his drumsticks, "Like the Big Easy." He snaps out a rim shot.

Red's handkerchief juggling increases, "We is a little off the Chit'lin Circuit, how is it, ya'll decided to come here?"

Hawkshaw, "We hope to offer something new to the colored community, especially in the South. We figure to start small. Let word of mouth sweep out across the land, that a new sound, a new calling for those who hear the message within." He taps his chest and smiles enigmatically.

The thin young man in a loose white shirt snorts in derision. Red glares at him as the diffident youth ambles back to the bar, "My sister's eldest boy." He shakes his head, "Aint' nuthin' but dewdropper."

Elvin, "Sleeps all d-day, do he?"

Red, "Yep. Dead to the world."

Elvin, "There may b-be, some hope for him yet." He smiles to himself. Red stares at him perplexed. Red's sister, Alma pokes her head out of the kitchen door and bellows at him, "You wanna keep your front door, you'd better head off the stampede outside." Then she ducks back into her kitchen cloister. Red mops his brow and waves his kerchief at her as he heads for the front door, "Well, everyone had better be wide awake now."

'T', "Been meanin' to ask you; what's with the cheaters?"

Elvin, "I think they m-make me look deceptively m-meek." He beams smugly. 'T' guffaws, "You think you sharp jus' cuz you head is pointed!" He laughs and shoves the bass player in a rough, but genial fashion and works his way up to the dais where his kit sits, now softly gleaming in the naked light of a few primitive 'specials' formed from coffee cans that are focused on the bandstand.

"Ah, honey, don't you go bein' no cancelled stamp," 'T' drawls as Ella orbits the bandstand on her convoluted way to the kitchen.

She stops, half turns, her chin over her shoulder, "Oh, I can deliver. You a thigh man or breast man?"

'T', "Ha! No BBQ for me, sweet thing, but if you're offering up some pretty neck bones, I'll bite."

Hawkshaw, "Don't listen to him. He knows feeding before a show makes him logy. Can't use a drummer who's behind the beat."

'T', "Maybe later, darlin'. I'll have worked up an appetite by then." He rattles out a drum fill.

"You slay me," Ella giggles. "Ya'll just go on cuttin' yo' self a piece o' cake." And with that she slides away at angle that allows her big brown eyes to linger on the cheeky musician.

Elvin fidgets and crosses to Hawkshaw, "Think the restless nativists would like to serve us some serious b-b-barbeque?"

Hawkshaw merely smiles and continues with his tinkering at the keyboard.

Elvin, "Think they know?" He leans in, his face a mask of anxiety.

Hawkshaw shakes his head, "Nothing we can't handle." He hits a tonic chord and pops up from the bench, "It's what they don't know that'll get 'em." He pats the bass players cheek playfully and moves to collect his horn.

The barkeep mutters this as Ella passes, "You know ain't nuthin' good gonna come o' your kitin' around with no big city cheese."

Ella, "Oowee, listen to tha wannabe drugstore cowboy." And she slams her way through the double doors into the kitchen, narrowly missing Red who is on his way out.

Barkeep shakes his lowered head as he scrubs too hard at the surface of the bar with his towel,"Same ol' bad."

Red looks back at his retreating waitress, then returns his gaze to the bandstand," No smoking, no drinking and not one of them's been to the kitchen," he shakes his head. "Queerest musicians I ever seen."

"They's all dry", the barkeep pouts as he wipes irritably at the bar surface.

"I wouldn't go that far," Hawkshaw interjects as he scoots by.

"Just toss them some raw meat," Chessie offers as she thumps the double swinging doors into the kitchen.

The night sky is dark and as soaked with stars as the land is with water. The Milky Way shimmers like a river in the firmament now that the clouds have dissipated. Frogs, toads, crickets, all croak and chitter/chatter making for a dark and lulling orchestra. The moon is brilliant, blazing back lighting for the bats to wheel before. The bluish flames of Will o' the wisps dance and flicker across the murky landscape.

Evangeline is dragging a half-asleep Thad into the space she shares with Lula Mae. She thrusts him forward and he totters to the obviously empty bed. The sight serves to rouse him slightly and he frowns and turns to Evangeline, "Been a while since she's sleepwalked." He crosses to the door and looks out. Then he turns back to the girl, "Let me get something on my feet and get a lantern ready."

Outside the Red Tide, the walls are reverberating with *Boogie Woogie*.

Inside all three band members have taken turns with vocals and various instruments to augment and vary their sound. Often from number to number. All distinctive in their style and timbre their voices flavor each song differently, but Elvin's is the most remarkable as his daily speech impediment is nowhere to be heard once his voice is riding a propulsive beat.

Elvin:

"I may be wrong, but I won't be wrong always,
You gonna long for me baby one of these rainy days.
She got ways like a devil, she shaped like a frog,
Start to lovin' me I holler Ooh goddog…."

Elvin's hands scamper across the face of his instrument like contrapuntal spiders on the same web, a copacetic tarantella that carried the deep thrum, breast felt between the thump of the bass drum.

King Oliver's 'Black Bottom Stomp' gets a frenetic treatment. Cries of, "Get hot! Get hot!" egged on the loose-limbed dancers, glowing with effort and unalloyed exultation of the conjunction of their ecstatic motion and the music. Hands shoot out, legs flail and fly. Every few minutes a lithe doxy would be hoisted aloft and be flung about in peerless arcs and returned to terra firma with equal aplomb.

On *Everybody Loves My Baby* Elvin takes up the banjo and Hawkshaw the bandoneon as 'T' belts out the lyrics in a gravelly shout:

> Now when my baby kisses me
> Upon my rosy cheeks
> I just let those kisses be
> Don't wash my face for weeks!

Ella is primping her hair in Chessie's mirror which is mottled with moisture and cracked with age. Barkeep slips up behind her and tries to embrace her. She gives a small cry of dismay and wriggles out of his grasp.

Barkeep, "A c'mon, baby, don't-"

"Di, mi, but ain't you the monkey's eyebrows...." Ella says as she pushes him away and makes for the rear entrance.

After not more than ten minutes after scouring the locations where Lula Mae would frequent in her somnambulistic state and finding no trace of her, Thad in his yellow rain slicker and hat, groans with the effort to even reach down to grasp the crank starter handle on has 1912 Model T delivery truck. Considering the area both in terms of topography and location it didn't get a lot of use. And it takes several attempts before the engine catches. Evangeline sits in the passenger seat and grips the edge of the wooden door frame, white-knuckled with apprehension.

7

I n a scraggly thicket three hundred yards from the roadhouse, by the light of a dozen rattletrap vehicles, Wallace and his minions gather, readjusting hoods and robes. Shotguns dangle from ham-like fists, six shooters being stuffed into belts, jugs still being passed around, but surreptitiously. Dogs and horses reel about clamoring, roused by all the commotion of their two-legged counterparts.

Corky, still drunk, "I can't see out of the eye holes." He pulls at the pointed hood, this way and that, "If'n I get this eye lined up then this one just-"

Wallace, "I told you to get an official one, not the one your mother made."

"But, Wallace, I don' tol' you, I ain't got the scratch for that kinda-"

Wallace snatches the elongated mask from Corky and holds it out for everyone to see and hisses, "Three years ago leadership finally got wise and started treating it's agenda as a serious business. It has spread far and wide because our cause has been codified and discipline is paramount because make no mistake, we are at war. We are the backbone of this great nation's destiny and it is we who will make it stand tall for it's promises."

He shoves the offending piece of garment back into Corky's mortified grasp. He stalks towards the direction of the roadhouse and stares for a moment, then turns and addresses his legion, "Them that has can ride, others walk. Lester, get the dogs back in the trucks. Bring 'em up fast once the festivities start."

"How far afield of the law we gonna get tonight?" One of the dutiful asks Wallace nervously as they slowly nudge their mounts quietly.

Wallace responds while looking out towards the potential mayhem, "Necessity knows no law. Except the strongest survives." He windmills his arm forward and his ramshackle, but homogenized band slouches onward.

It is almost the midnight hour. The musicians are drifting back after taking a break between sets. 'T' comes back from behind the building, wiping his mouth with the back of his hand, a little stagger to his swagger, eyes red-rimmed. Red watches him go by, "Ya'll always toke up between sets?"

Red's sister comes out of the kitchen to take in the scene as she wipes her hands on her soiled and well worn apron.

"No worries on that account. We don't truck with that kinda tea," Hawkshaw says as he passes them on his way to the bandstand.

She scowls at the obviously buzzed percussionist, then at Red and bangs back through the double doors into the kitchen. Red shakes his head and wiping at his matching apron follows her.

'T' settles behind his drum kit, twirls his drumsticks in his hands like propellers on an airplane, "I's ready, I's ready, I's ready!"

Ella slams in through the back door of the club and staggers into the nearest wall. She stands, one hand resting on her thigh the other on the wall. Her breathing is ragged and she weaves unsteadily as she emits small grunts with the effort to stay upright.

The Barkeep, who has been keeping a weather eye out for her since he watched her slinking out the back door, sees her and rushes to her side, "Damn, you half cut, or what?"

She falls against him. He tries to gather her in his arms when she suddenly straightens up, takes his face in her hands and kisses him deeply. Shocked, he tries to pull away, but her teeth are locked on his lower lip and he escapes with a yelp, "What the hell...? "She staggers away. He looks after her then he feels something on his hands. He holds them up in the dim, smoky light: they glisten with a dark burgundy colored liquid. A sudden crash of cymbals jars his attention back to the main room where-

There is sonic madness. Wild stomps, thumping and crashing from the drums, 'Shake It and Break It', breaks out. Hawkshaw plucks the derby off of 'T's head and uses it as a mute for his horn, then plays keep away with it from 'T with Elvin when his solo is finished. The crowd joins in the good humored games with laughter and encouraging shouts.

Elvin suddenly stops, mid stride and cocks his head towards the ceiling. His nostrils flare as he cranes his head in an arc. "I smell smoke and it ain't no bar-b-que," he calls to his rhythm section partner.

"Time for the Night Tripper," 'T' responds as he tosses his drumsticks into the audience and slips a specialized pair of sticks from the holder rigged to his bass drum.

Wallace stands, arms akimbo, fists on hips as he watches orange flames and black smoke surge from the rear of the Red Tide clubhouse.

Corky, "It's the Choctaw boys, Wally. They got no more sense than-"

Just then a shout nearby interrupts them, "Burn them niggers out!"

Wallace doesn't wait to hear the rest, but brushes past Corky and stalks to one Klansman who is swaying drunkenly on his feet and guffawing with each round he squeezes off in the direction of the patrons who attempt to flee through the front entrance. Wallace spins the shooter around and snatches the pistol from his hand and shoves him to the ground," We're not here not here to spread fire, but to spread the word, to spread fear. That's our purifying flame. Let them go and tell the others."

Hawkshaw catches the signal from 'T' and deliberately turns to face the draped mirror, gathers himself and emits a piercing tone that causes the entire crowd to recoil in unison like a single-celled creature. All dancing and conversation stops and many patrons hold their ears. Suddenly, Hawkshaw escaltes to a note that causes the canvas over the mirror to tremble and ripple. Then, with a crash, the mirror shatters and the shards cascade to the floor. Even though the canvas keeps any pieces from hurling outward, those in the vicinity shriek and flee the bar area.

'T' and Elvin slide along the back wall and off of the bandstand as the customers squeal and rush about like frightened rodents. Hawkshaw catches the eyes of his band mates and nods for them to separate. They return nods in acknowledgment and 'T' heads for the front door as Elvin squeezes his way to the kitchen. They both start to drag patrons with them and shout above the din, "This way! This way!"

Most of the panicked patrons respond to the two musician and start to scramble after them to the exits. Elvin meets Red at the kitchen door, "I'll see everyone gets out this way what c-can. Get your sister to watch the b-back door and get outside yourself and get a b-bucket brigade goin'."

Red looks anxiously at the chaos and smoke filling the dance floor, but then nods in compliance and scurries out the door. Elvin holds the swinging doors to the kitchen open and gestures for the stampede to pass him. He uses one arm to hold open the door and the other to keep the herd from trampling one another, "Slow d-down! Take it easy!"

Chessie marches stolidly past him, her purse slung over her shoulder. She and Elvin lock eyes for a moment before she passes through the doorway and heads in the opposite direction of the other patrons. Elvin feels something like a chill run through him from the contact, then he too slips outside.

Chessie continues at her own measured gait towards the West side of the building where Red's car is always parked. She slings her purse into the passenger seat and crosses around to the driver's side. As she passes the rear of the car she see's that the spare tire cover lies on the ground. She frowns and picks it up. Then as she goes to put it back in place she notices a small swatch of grimy fabric snagged on one of the cover's fasteners. She straightens up and peers about as if scenting the air. Then she tosses the cover away and strides quickly towards the thickest part of the tree line.

Angry clouds are gathering, seemingly without a gust of wind and add a pall to the scene along with the thick, black, acrid smoke scudding from the clubhouse.

Wallace sniffs the air," Kerosene", he growls.

Fellow KKK members are flocking like giant cranes and harassing or grasping at the fleeing club patrons. Shrieks and yells surge amidst the crackling of the flames. Red's nephew finds himself hemmed in by half a dozen hooded foes and starts to fight back, but gets swarmed. "We only need one guest for our necktie party," Wallace says to no one in particular.

'T' comes tumbling out of the billowing smoke and directly into the mob assaulting the barkeep. His momentum takes them down like bowling pins. Wallace, "And look what Providence delivers," he says as he strides up to 'T'. The drummer barely gets to his feet, when Wallace pistol whips him with his gun butt and drops him to his knees. Wallace grabs his victim's collar and bellows to his troops, "Look at this bastardization of his own inferior race. Let's do his community a favor and put it out of it's misery."

"Look, there's a fire!" Evangeline shouts above the racket and sputter of the four cylinder engine. Thad switches off the motor and they glide into a small hollow. When they come to rest, they hear whooping and hollering and the sound of sporadic gunfire. Evangeline starts to bolt towards the sound, but Thad holds her back. He places his finger to his lips and leads her on a slow creep forward to the clearing.

Once they reach the edge of the trees, the vista before them is thrown in stark relief by the light of the full moon, which peeps through gathering clouds. The most prominent features, though are three crosses around twelve feet tall with flames crackling and leaping from them, throwing a quivering gleam on the white clad figures that mill and lurch around in the mud and oats and vasey grass.

Evangeline looks from the burning crosses to the white-robed specters. She notices that on the left breast of their garments the form of the cross is reiterated. Thad blurts out in apprehension as he looks around, "What on earth would have prompted Lula Mae to come out here? Are you sure-"

Just then a dark horse with a rider followed by a ragged faction, flails along over the sodden ground, emerging from the darkness. Evangeline gasps as she recognizes the band's drummer-tethered to the horse by a length of rope and dragging him behind. 'T' stumbles along, hands bound together through a gauntlet of the draped, flapping tribe who kick and flail at him. Some even lift their hoods enough to spit at him.

The rider reins up near the only substantial oak tree in then area. 'T' tumbles to the ground and lies there, his shoulders heaving with effort. A thin, shabby looking member reels up to Wallace.

Corky,"What do you do with something you want to dry out? Hang it on a line." He pushes his way through the throng and hauls 'T' to his feet. "Right, Wally?" he hiccups.

The lead rope is removed from the saddle and is launched over a low, sturdy branch of the tree. Once the end is retrieved, it is presented to Corky and only then does Evangeline see that it has already been fastened into a noose. It takes three Klansmen to loop the noose over the struggling musician's head as Corky re-attaches the rope to the horse's saddle. 'T' manages to shrug the mob off of him, but Wallace leans over his own mount and spurs the tethered plug into motion with a slap of his hand on the horse's flank.

The nag springs forward forward until his rider and his two-legged fetter bring him to a writhing halt. 'T' is lifted ten feet into the air, thrashing at the end of the noose like a gigged catfish. His body jackknifes in the air, knees jerking up to his chest, "Aaaah! Oh! Oh! Aaarggh!"

For what seems an eternity, the grotesque display lingers on, eyes bulging, a red froth working out of his mouth that now only produces gurgles and grunts. Thad and Evangeline clutch at each other, she buries her head into his ample side and he claps a hand over his eyes.

"Sweet Jesus!" Wallace hears one of the members next to him moan in apparent sympathy. He looks around and notices that some of the Klan are starting to look away or fidget restlessly.

"This is taking too long",Wallace utters. He spies two members taking no longer furtive slugs from a jug almost as if they could anesthetize themselves from the gruesome spectacle. As one chugs the other mewls,

"Aw, don't soak up all o' the panther piss." The closest fellow member offers, "I could go get the kerosene."

Wallace says, "No", and spurs his horse forward and snags the jug from the pair and moves to the member closest to the heaving, macabre proceeding. He tosses the jug to his startled associate and bellows, "Speed up the process!" He goads his mount up to the tree where the drummer swings in eccentric arcs. Wallace spurs his horse at the quaking minion who then takes both hands and shakes the jug at the lurid pendulum, splashing the high octane corn liquor everywhere.

"What he gotta waste good liquor, like that for?" one of the deprived pair moans.

"It's for the 'Cause', cuz," the other says with more than a trace of bitterness.

Wallace, "We forgot to get the name of the guest of honor for tonight's festivities."

The member closest to Wallace steps forward with his torch, "Ah, hell, lets' just call him 'Crispy'", drawls the hooded wag as he slowly lifts the torch towards 'T's as he continues to sway under the creaking branch.

T, "They call me, Mr. Tibbs!" he bellows as the torch strikes him. This causes a renewed round of painful howling as flames sputter to life across his tattered clothing. The hooligan with the torch steps forward to goad the fire on, but then-

A sudden shock wave blares out of the copse of nearby river birch and dogwood. A cleaving timbre shatters the night air and drives the mob, hands clasped to their ears, staggering in circles or to their knees in agony. Those holding torches drop them, or struggle to hold them up. Wallace's horse rears and plunges, wailing in pain and fright much like it's rider. The blood hounds howl and whirl away into the trees.

Hawkshaw comes riding out of the thicket on a pale steed like an avenging angel, with an ivory object to his lips. From something that resembles a tusk erupts a crystal, clarion blast that rips through the air before it. Some sheets are scattering to the winds, flapping like sails in a squall. Others are spread-legged, heads swiveling trying to get a bearing on the sound. Two other horses, cut loose from their riders help Hawkshaw and his mount form a wedge that tears through and sunders the assembly.

Evangeline and Thad wince and groan. They cover their ears and try to stagger away only to have Thad stumble into a tree trunk and drop in a faint. Evangeline doesn't notice. She ends up kneeling on the ground, hunched over, hands clasped over her ears. The sky shudders with thunder and the stars are now almost obliterated by dark and lowering clouds that begin to besprinkle the scene.

Tibbs has broken his bonds and is gripping the noose with both hands. He swings down and hooks one foot under Corky's chin and plants the other on the back of his neck. With a convulsive wrench, he hauls Corky into the air and begins a rhythmic rocking. Cackling malevolently, he makes Corky a bawling pendulum over the melee. The flames still flicker across his desiccated clothing as he trails smoke like a sky-writer.

One Klansman has managed to fumble a shotgun out from his ponderous robe and trains it on Hawkshaw. A whistling sound slices the air. A metal cord whips around the muzzle of the side-by-side and is wrenched away from the gunsel who is sent sprawling. A high-pitched giggle spills out of the darkness. The prone hooligan gets to his knees when a wavering shadow forms behind him and whips the hood off of his head. Alarmed, he scrambles to his feet to face his tormentor, but the shadow has bolted behind him again. A bass string loops over his head and around his neck. He claws at the tightening garrote as he is lifted off of his feet and Elvin's face slides into view next to his, tittering with ghastly glee.

Corky, now whining in alarm, is made to swoop back and forth across the night sky. With a loud grunt, Tibbs releases Corky on the upswing and sends him in a keening arc into the darkness where he lands with a sickening thud. "This is for Tulsa, ofay!" Tibbs hurls himself with a rattling snarl onto the back of one of the hysterical, hooded henchmen. The clearing has become a hell-pit of blood-stained sheets, scattering in the air like confetti on New Years. Screams of terror are often abruptly truncated by roars or growls one might only expect to hear on the savannahs of Africa.

Hawkshaw lowers his horn and gives a howl, arching back in his saddle as if baying to the ash blonde moon. First Tibbs, then Elvin also lift their heads in utterance of an ensuing strain that is even more piercing and terrifying than the horn. After a few seconds the mingling pitches create an overtone, a sympathetic vibration that seems to pierce all of the solid objects in the clearing. Even the trees tremor and the leaves hiss as their boughs shimmy together.

The clearing is is rapidly becoming vacated of the soiled sheets that infested it. Tibbs, still smoldering and looking like a thing loosed from the everlasting fire, reaches into what is left of his trouser waistband and pulls out two drumsticks and twirls them in in the air. They make a sharp whistling sound from the finely tapered ends they as they revolve. He rears back and let's fly with one of them, nailing a fleeing figure in the throat. He yelps with exuberance, then squats and launches himself twenty feet through the air and lands on another victim bringing the other drumstick down hard into his prey's neck.

The coagulated clouds resound with thunder, lightning strikes stab the ground. The hanging tree explodes as a bolt smites the oak wood and launches flaming shrapnel. A huge spherical void in the branches crackles with flame that makes it seem a giant precursor to the crosses. Rain starts to fall and the damped white robes now are streaked with now are streaked with red.

Tibbs," Now you gonna see the real Night Rider!" "The real Imperial Nighthawk!" enjoins Elvin as Hawkshaw bulldogs Wallace down from his horse. His lips pulled back in a rictus of elation, Hawkshaw raises the horn in one hand and Wallace in the other. Burson squirms and sputters at the end of his arm. Hawk plunges the tusk into Wallace's neck, lifts him even higher and funnels the crimson flow into his mouth from the horn.

Tibbs, "That's for Tulsa, ofay!" bellows as he hurls a shrieking, flailing Klan member into the burning cross. It snaps with a resounding crack and flaming chunks of wood erupt and scatter to the damp ground echoing the stricken tree.

"And that's for Philips County, c-c-crackers!" Elvin hollers as he lashes freely with bull fiddle strings in both hands at any Ku Kluxer that is unfortunate enough to blunder into his reach in the turmoil.

Tibbs grins as he limps towards his fellow rhythm section player. "Roll, tide, roll!"

"'B-b-bama crimson tide!", Elvin hollers as the watches the dregs of the terrorists disappear into the dark.

Hawk tosses Wallace's carcass from the saddle and reins in the mount. He trots the horse over to his compatriots. They are the only figures now visible within view.

"I thought you'd never get here," Tibbs says as they meet. He is stained red from dirt and blood.

Elvin checks the wound around the drummer's neck; the vertebrae are exposed, "That's gonna a few days to heal."

Hawkshaw, "Keeping the audience waiting just increases the suspense."

Elvin, "I think they was a little p-p-preoccupied to n-n-n-notice."

Hawkshaw, "Not them... them." The others turn to follow his pointing finger. Their gaze is directed to the stand of trees where Thad begins to stir into consciousness. As they start in that direction, they hear Thad shriek. The three of them rush to the site. They find Eva still crumpled on the ground, but recovering. Elvin checks the store owner, "He's just fainted."

Then Tibbs spies another figure at the edge of the thicket, "Oh, have mercy, no...." He looks past Eva to a small crumpled mass under a dogwood. Tibbs moves quickly to Lula Mae, who lies unconcious. A crescent of blood soaks her side. Tibbs, "Dammit!"

Elvin joins him and gently places a hand on her tiny chest. He looks up at Hawkshaw, "She-"

"I know, I see it," the band leader cuts him short. Just then, Evangeline brushes past him and throws herself opposite Elvin at Lula Mae's side. She quivers as she looks down, then looks back over her shoulder at Hawkshaw with pleading eyes. She wails, and goes into hysterics, her small hands clawing at the blood soaked red clay. Her mind's eye conjures up a brief vista of her and Lula Mae's initial contact. She feels her heart burst now just as it had then. Hawkshaw snatches her up and holds her. She flails against him at first, but his strength is prodigious. He holds her out from him and commands, "Look at me! Look at me! What do you see?"

She stops squirming and with a sharp intake of breath locks eyes with him and her body starts to go slack. Then her gaze hovers past his shoulder as she expounds in a distracted fashion, "Granny.... Granny said we'd always be.... be together...."

"You is balled up if you think this is gonna be real help. You talkin' 'bout a child. An innocent in the ways o' this world or any other," Tibbs warns.

Elvin, "Someone who's always gonna b-b-be a little girl."

Hawkshaw, "That's why it has to be her choice."

Then he turns his head to follow the child's dreamy gaze. Chessie stands among the shadows of the dogwood. They seem to share a mutual acknowledgment before Hawkshaw nods and turns back to Evangeline.

Elvin, his hand still on Lula Mae's breast urges, "Time's a wastin'."

Hawkshaw, "It's up to you. You really want to be together that bad?" he says as he gives her a little shake. This brings Evangeline back to present awareness and she nods furiously and wipes at her eyes.

Hawkshaw takes her hands from her eyes and locks them again in a mutual stare, "In this world sometimes when you pick something up you have to sacrifice something else to balance the load. Give up, sun, warmth, babies, etc."

"Childhood", Elvin offers. Hawkshaw snaps at him over his shoulder, "Everyone has to do that." He turns back to Evangeline whose gaze has not faltered. She gives a small, but definite nod. Hawkshaw looks at her grimly, then say, "All right."

Hawkshaw nods to Tibbs to take Lula Mae. Hawk bounces Evangeline gently in his arms. Her sobs have turned to hiccups. He tells her to look at Lula Mae," She's sleeping. Soon you will be, too." After a moment he touches her chin to bring her gaze back to him. She asks "Will I be damned to everlasting hellfire?"

Hawk, "There's many who'd say: yes. But, un-dead means: who really knows?"

He shifts her to the crook of his arm, "Now", he turns her face to his and she falls deep into his eyes again. When her eyes are at half-mast, he takes his free hand and raises it to his mouth and tears at his wrist with his sharp teeth. He then brings his oozing veins under her nose. She sniffs and recoils at first, but he persists, waving the blood under her nose until, mouth watering, she succumbs. He head drops forward and her mouth finds his arm. Then after a few moments, she begins to suckle, then she reaches up, one hand around his neck, the other clamps on his forearm as she begins to feed in earnest.

Tibbs lifts Lula Mae in his arms and is about to perform the same ritual on the tiny child, when Elvin grabs his arm and stops him. He stoops and picks up a small object from the ground. It is Grannys' gris-gris. He holds it up for inspection and in doing so catches Chessie's eye. She nods to him and he nods back. He gently unfolds one of the girl's dainty hands and places it in her palm and closes her fingers around it. He looks up to Chessie for approval, but she has vanished.

Tibbs starts to move slowly away as he sinks his sharp teeth into his own wrist and applies it to the seemingly lifeless body of Lula Mae.

Elvin, "All Saints Day tomorrow."

Tibbs, "So?"

Elvin, "Custom dictates I get the back."

"Damn, you hard as lard!" Tibbs exclaims as he tilts the child's head back further to help induce the waxy liquid further into her gullet. "Hawk, you tell 'em!"

Hawkshaw sighs to himself, "You can take the boy out of the church, but…." Then over his shoulder, "The young ladies get the best accommodations tonight." He turns back to Evangeline and removes her hold on his arm and lifts away his wrist. Her eyes are glazed and bloodshot, her mouth glutted crimson. He presses his wrist to his mouth and with a few rasping passes of his tongue manages a seal for the wound. He looks down at the young girl and places his long fingers tenderly over her face, then softly draws them away, drawing down the curtains of her eyes.

8

DAY OF THE DEAD

Evangeline can feel her eyelids open, but there is nothing for her eyes to capture. She starts to feel panic well up in her when she hears a distant male voice in a husky whisper trolling:

"Before this time another year, I may be gone
It's our lonesome graveyard, oh Lord how long?
God sent Noah, the rainbow sign,
Said no more water the fire next time."

She cannot tell if his voice is reaching her ears or is already inside her head. The sound starts to squelch as if water is flowing into her ears. Somewhere a faint green luminosity like sunlight through deep water plays on her retinas. Or maybe it is just a memory of light projected on the scrim of her mind's eye. A long silhouette wavers before her as it turns and trains two red eyes upon her. The singing is faint now, a tiny echo from a great distance. The music is sweet, but she feels bitter cold coming upon her.

She feels as if she is floating upwards through dark water. In the distance she can make out a path of light. It grows larger, brighter. A sky balloons with clouds. And an object is coming towards her. The image is translucent and wavering. She feels a change in the pressure around her as she seems to reach a surface. The object now solidifies into her mirror image. They hover within inches of each other. Suddenly, Evangeline's point of view shifts and she can see now from a distance the two images, both floating in darkness.

Eva rolls her eyes to heaven in spasms of pain. A flash of white light explodes between her eyes and she sees an obsidian sky. The stars are diamonds on a navy blue velvet pinwheel. They arc in fits and starts overhead. As they spiral across the sky, her distress seems to travel away from her. From the earth. The stars seem to be coming closer. Closer. It seems as if they should be brushing her cheeks, flocking her eyelashes like snowflakes.

Suddenly, she is looking down. She sees her body in repose, eyes closed, arms crossed over her chest. She is in a yellow dress with scalloped white trim that fluctuates like sea foam. She has a sensation of floating away from this vision. Her still, white, shimmering body recedes from her sight and then she feels and thinks no more.

Rhythmic clapping sounds slap and clatter in her ears. Her eyelids creak open, but her vision is blurry, the light is too intense for her to bear, so she squeezes them shut again. But, she cannot shut out the many voices that ring out in a call and response:

> "God sent Gabriel (How long?), Behind the alter (How long),
> Pick up your trumpet (How long?), begin to blow it (How long?),
> I want ya to blow it (How long?), nice and even (How long?),
> Pick up your children (How long?), lay down your sleeping loud as thunder (How long?)
> Wake up them sinners (How long?), they roll on under (How long?)"

Then the slow sensation of rocking as a faint sound murmurs up from inside: "Hush, hush chile. You is watched." Suddenly, she writhes in spasm and she can envision herself – drenched and shivering in a blanket.

She takes another chance and squints and sees Chessie's substantial breasts framing her scowling countenance as Granny hovers over her shoulder. A soothing, cooing sound emanates from them as a warm hand brushes the matted locks on her forehead. Then as suddenly as this vision presents itself, it is swept away by another spasm of pain and darkness.

Dusk. Evangeline still hears a dim echo of the earlier voices:

"Wake up my preacher, lay down their sleeping,
Wake up my deacon, lay down your weeping,
Wake up my memory, lay down your trembling,
Wake up them children, lay down their sleeping,
How long, How long? How long…?"

She senses change, her skin begins to prickle with a chill. The voices echo and overlap, losing synch causing a cacophonous reverberation. Evangeline wakes with a start. She is lying on her back. Her eyes swim into focus on the fricative branches of an enormous silver elm tree overhead. Her head lolls to one side. She spies Hawkshaw's hat jauntily perched on a headstone. Then the light begins to sting and burn her eyes. The sun just now dips below the horizon.

Freezing, shivering. Then, she feels heat, her face flushes and some scent fills her nose and mouth and causes her teeth to throb. Her mouth waters and her tongue recalls and smells blood. There is something familiar – a globe of warmth feels pressed against her cheek. She instinctively turns her head towards the source. Gradually she swoons into consciousness.

Her mouth waters and she feels a twisting convulsion rising from her gut. Spasms start to wrack her. "Is this dying? Mother? Father? Am I dying?" She feels these thoughts in her own voice as they shriek across her mind. Suddenly she flashes on an image: Chessie standing in a white enamel tub with a white towel that turns red. Her hair, also wrapped in a towel, skin with a patina like bronze. The tub is filling from below with a dark liquid. To the side she sees Hawkshaw hold the snake up and look it in the eyes. It almost seems as if he would play it like his own horn. A hissing sound seems to be coming from the snake that fills the room. The tub is now overflowing and Chessie has dropped her towel and spreads her arms. Hawkshaw turns to her and says," The night turns the world upside down and people inside out."

Evangeline screws up her courage and flutters open her eyes. A female head is silhouetted above her. The pale, violet light forms a corona around it. A hand stretches out of the shadows and offers her an effulgent fruit, glowing a warm crimson from deep inside it's translucent skin. It seems more like a gem than food. All at once her nostrils fill with an aroma that prompts mouth secretions and wipes all reasoning from her mind. She snatches at the object and with jaws wide enough to make a snake envious, she bites heavily and greedily into the fruit, over and over again, heedless of the juice that slavers over her face, chest and hands, the warm, sweet sensation, the coppery taste. Thick liquid sensations.

Granny's voice trickles into her ears,"You is watched. You chose a thorny path, but remember: jus' cuz you was born again to th' dark, don't mean you have t' live there." Her spasms subside and the world comes rushing in crowding her senses. Evangeline looks up and Granny's impassive face swims into focus. Then her visage quickly morphs into that of Lula Mae's doll. It whispers intensely in Lula Mae's voice to her, "Hurry, hurry!" hisses the voice. "Let's give up all the other worlds except the one where we belong. Even in the dark we will know each other. You are not without love, the dark will be our womb tonight."

She feels extremely sated and drowsy, almost to the point of fading back to unconsciousness, but her eyes will not completely close. Past the branches of the elm tree, she watches as the night descends like indigo amber-the stars set, fixed, frozen, distant. The moon is a cold, ivory sickle. After a while – minutes? hours?-light flares at the corner of her vision. Her head slumps to one side.

Ten feet away, the headlights of the hearse sculpt the fluted trunk of the old silver maple tree in the graveyard. In the ambient light she can make out the bass fiddle case lying on the ground next to the driver's door. It starts to rock slightly and fitfully, then it shudders to an upright position and rocks to a stop. Then the clasps all open in a series of syncopated snaps and the lid flips open.

Scrunched inside is what looks to be the mangled corpse of Tibbs. Then with a groan, his back arches and he sits up stiffly in the case. His arms were entwined over his head in order to accommodate the dimensions of the container. Now he untwists them with much cracking and crunching of cartilage and bone as they slowly drop to his sides. He stands and gives himself a good shaking all over and after a few grunts of relief and satisfaction, opens his eyes, gives a big yawn and starts to move forward out of the ambient light, humming and flexing his musculature. He probes his neck wound lightly as he moves slowly off.

She hears the creaking of wood and metal. She can see the coffin in the back of the hearse through the window. It's lid slams shut and Elvin emerges from the back. He reaches into his breast pocket and withdraws his glasses and puts them on. After adjusting his collar, he moves off in the same direction as the drummer.

Hawkshaw, "Not what you had, but what are you prepared to do with what you've got. Any good musician knows that." She startles slightly as he suddenly appears and hunkers down beside her. He reaches into the breast pocket of his shirt and withdraws – a harmonica. He smiles, then brings it to his lips and blows a short riff, then holds it out to her, jiggling it temptingly in his fingers.

Evangeline is confused about her current situation. As she is slow to respond a wizened face appears over Hawkshaw's shoulder:

Granny, "No sense in just lyin' there like a jellyfish wid da misery. Ya'll don't want to be late for your little friend."

Hearing the obvious reference to Lula Mae, Evangeline experiences a swell of feeling that lifts her head. Only then does she realize it has been resting in Cheesie's lap. In the background Evangeline can hear Granny's soft, cracking voice humming as she limps away with a cane. The humming slides into a soft murmured phrase, "Can't no grave hold my body down."

E vangeline feels a rocking motion again. It makes her wake with a start. Her eyes adjust quickly to the dark and she sees the wood grain of the trunk lid just inches from her face. She sniffs and scents the sun still peeking over the horizon. She closes her eyes again and settles back with a relieved sigh. They were on their way.

In a moment the sun would be down and she would be free to stroll around the length of the ancient twenty-five foot foot keel boat Thad had purchased after selling the dry goods store. "Just the right size for the three of us", Evangeline thought as she squirmed in anticipation. "Especially since Lula Mae and I take so little room both for us and our needs."

After the night of the fire and it's aftermath, the three of them decided to move on. Actually, the decision was kind of made for them once the others arrived. Lethe is mostly abandoned now, by not just the white folk. Fight turned to flight for both races. It was a struggle to find anyone to sell the store to or help them load the boat until Red made an offer and Granny convinced a few of the more capable community members to help.

Evangeline flicks at the trunk lid and it pops up smartly into place. She hoists herself out of the box and onto her feet with one swift movement. She still marveled at the actions she could perform now. But, she and Lula Mae had agreed to keep their new found powers in check around her uncle. He had a way of becoming quite anxious when he would see them carrying a trunk with uncanny ease that would tax the strength of two grown men, let alone a prepubescent child.

Was it really only three days ago that she sat at dusk, trying to play her new harmonica, waiting for Lula Mae? She was always a late riser. She found her new set of incisors got in the way. "You"ll get then hang of it, don't you worry none. In fact, you can get some pretty sweet effects once used to using them," Hawkshaw reassured her just before he took his leave.

Responding as if hearing Evangeline's initiate attempts on the instrument, Lula Mae made her nocturnal debut. She seemed as Evangeline did, entirely composed regarding her current state. The only concern was that their relationship continued and that no one could put asunder.

Thad turns from the tiller, "Where to?"

Evangeline purses her lips in thought as her eyes flicker out across the water for some moments, "Granny says I been to Beelutherhatchee and back and that will make me strong." Her hips rock back and forth slightly as she ponders the question. Then, "So, I guess, just wherever the water takes us."

"Maybe someday go to Birmingham, KC, Chitown even New York," Evangeline pronounces. Then to herself she whispers, "Some of those places Hawk told me – well, maybe not told, but shared with me – sights, sounds, thoughts." She can still hear the call of trumpet and voices. A call down the ages for freedom from oppression.

"This town never had much use for us any way. Doesn't miss the pot-bellied stove, cold doesn't bother me any more. Two small boxes and a cot on a raft. What else could our small tribe need?", she thoughfully continued as she turns to look back at the now almost deserted hamlet. Like the city of Jericho and so many other places that Providence felt the need to scratch from the earth.

Lula Mae nudges Evangeline from behind. The late riser. She nods towards the north shore. Evangeline follows her gaze and through the purple haze of twilight can just make out a tall, solid figure slowly striding into the river. She squints and suddenly her vision zooms into the point to where she can see the moisture glistening on Chessie's naked body and from the scales of the snake around her neck. Standing up to her waist in the river, she seems to be staring at the opposite shore. Then as the light continues to incrementally dim, she slowly strides forward until only her head and the snake's is visible. Then as the twilight winks on, they vanish below the subzero blue waters. Lula Mae cocks her arm gives a small wave. Evangeline dips her shoulder behind her friend and slips an arm around her tiny waist.

Thad looks at them mournfully, "You're not my little girls any more." He reaches out to adjust the ribbon in Lula Mae's hair, "Whatchyoo sayin' good-bye to? That dingy ol' backwater?"

Lula Mae doesn't respond, but Evangeline shakes her head and without turning says softly, "No."

Thad cranes his neck and peers in the same direction as the girls, but shrugs and leans his elbow back on the tiller, "Well whatever it is, I can't see it. Too dark."

"No. He can't", thought Evangeline. And for some reason it made her smile. Then she thinks to look inland and – yes, there; above where the thickest and gnarliest oaks grow, a thin line of smoke dwindles up into the sky from Granny's flue.

Thad, "We're not gonna get much further tonight, it's getting too dark to be safe. You want we should tie up? I'll get the lamps ready inside and you can come in where it's light."

"No," Evangeline says again, louder this time. The two girls turn to each other and one grin heartens another and they beam at each other. Then Lula Mae slips from Evangeline's embrace, but slides her hand into her friend's and gives it a squeeze. She nods, then turns back to watch the only home she has ever known recede almost beyond her vision.

Evangeline watches her fondly for a few moments, then she calls out, "Don't worry, Uncle. I'll be your leadsman. I'm going up front." Lula Mae smiles and nods, sagely, "You don't have to be afraid of the dark no more. "Evangeline nods and smiles in acknowledgment, "Now I love the night. I can see so much more than I used to. It feels strong. It feels free. It feels like…. like walls tumbling down."

THE CAPE

J erry is flying.

Hovering over the racks of jackets and suits in his father's haberdashery, he wonders why the lighting seems so dim. Ah, it must be a dream. He also wonders if, as in all his other flying dreams he would suddenly awaken if he tries to fly higher. Not that there is much headroom in the shop to begin with, but then-this *is* a dream after all, isn't it?

Suddenly, he spies a pair of legs on the floor jutting out from behind the counter. Now he realizes why it seems dark, it *is* night. Around eight o' clock, June second, nineteen thirty two. Anxiously, arms spread, he glides closer, already dreading the sight of – his father; flat on his back, one hand clawing at his chest, the other convulsing in the air, his pallor blue-gray; his father's fatal coronary. Brought on by – light scrapes across his vision. There! In the doorway. A menacing, back-lit figure. The light spilling through the doorway increases. He's holding a gun, surely-

The thief. The thief who stole his father's life, their family's happiness... The figure turns and plunges through the door. Run. Run, you coward. You murderer. Justice is mighty and it perseveres when it comes to those who tear at the fabric of civilized society.

Movement below captures his eye. His father's extended hand reaches for him, his eyes wild and pleading. Jerry no longer wants to soar away. Away from the pain, the darkness, the struggle. He starts to strain to reach his father. He wants to go down. Down. But, he feels it happening...

The door does not close. Instead the glare increases and peels back the scene from his sight as-

Jerry's eyes slide open. He feels his heart in his clamped jaw. He's been grinding his teeth in his sleep again. He stretches and groans to expiate the echoes of a two-year old scenario. How long? How long does the ache continue to gnarl even ones repose? Rolling over on his side and thumbing the sleep, tears and sweat from his eyes he debates a glance at the alarm clock, afraid of the earliness of the hour. He supposes he should feel grateful for any sleep at all in this heat, but with dreams like those ...

He sighs and rolls his head around to check the time: only an hour before he was going to get up. He slowly levers himself up on the bed and stares stolidly at the small desk wedged between the bed and window. There is that correspondence that has been piling up...

With a grunt, Jerry heaves himself off of his dank mattress and shuffles to the desk, absently scratching at himself as he brushes listlessly through the ocean of pulp that threatens to swamp his Royal number ten. A heap of hastily scratched ideas and dialogue on myriad scraps of paper, letters, sketches, magazines, comic books, movie fanzines and novels finally defeats his already perfunctory search until he spies an envelope resting on the type bars of the typewriter. He picks it up, his finger tapping the corner with the return address marked National Allied Publications. Probably just another rejection. He sighs and replaces it in it's prominent, if slighted position.

He is about to turn back to bed when his sight is arrested this time by a slash of color in the blunted parchment pyramid that has been coagulating on his desk. Film idol trading cards hawked by tobacco companies as promotion devices almost camouflaged a small but, colorful placard: William Powell, Jack Barrymore, Ronald Coleman, Doug Fairbanks junior and senior, Clark Gable all sporting interchangeable mustaches.

He peels the thin plaques away from a red and blue tile with yellow lettering and smudges the thin film of dust from it's glossy surface, tracing ellipses across the bright hued endorsement for a long forgotten health elixir. A scene conjures in his mind of his father Mitchell at the kitchen table after supper with his youngest son. Even years after establishing his career as a clothier he would revisit his previous occupation as sign painter. With color wheels and paint swatches, his father eagerly explained the alchemy of light and texture, of complimentary and contrasting colors and how all his previous experience with paint allowed him to select the most interesting garments for his small second-hand shop.

Jerry frowned at the recollection. The pall of his dream nestled like a nest of brambles in his heart, ever ready to snag and prick him with rue. He gently places the sign back into its place of honor and suddenly feels that the magazine and the correspondence and everything else could just wait. Without a job or any real prospects (and if truth be told) little interest in finding regular work, he was something of a free (if chagrined) agent. In order to shake off the doldrums of life, both waking and sleeping, he felt a little weekday holiday might be in order. And who better to play hooky with than his partner in 'pulpdom', Joe.

They could take in an afternoon matinee and combine a little recreation with some inspiration. Not likely, for there were few films out now that seemed to appeal to their sense of the fantastic. And if nothing else they could 'brainstorm' on ideas such as keeping access to Glenville High's mimeograph machine and more importantly how to get people to actually accept the austere offering of their little magazine. With their compound perseverance their endeavors would pay off someday. They had to. Then their snide and condescending classmates and his athlete brothers, Harry and Leo would not only have to acknowledge but express the proper gratitude for their imaginative gifts. Grabbing a book and a few select papers, he started to get dressed with a new sense of purpose.

Minutes later, Jerry is marking his place in the ever-present novel in his hand as he rounds the driveway of his house to the curb and almost runs into-

Minerva, his oldest sister who stands in a brown, deep pleated skirt with a wide yoke, head cocked. The effect gives her the appearance of a be-spectacled owl, "Since I don't see a jacket or a tie, I can assume you are not enroute to a job interview?"

Jerry stops mid stride, "Ah, no I – I mean, I was just, uh-"

"-No reason to be flustered, it's not an inquisition." Her slight Lithuanian lilt sometimes made it seem otherwise to Jerry.

"Actually, I was on my way to Glenville, I-

"-Oh, Jerry not that-"

Jerry's face falls. She sighs, "Sorry. It just kind of slipped out."

Jerry almost unconsciously cocks the arm with his book behind his back. Minerva's head tilts opposite, "Well. So, any news on the publication front?"

Jerry's mind flickers across images of the unopened envelope on his typewriter, the stacks of back issues of 'Science Fiction' and 'Cosmic Stories' moldering in his mother's garage. His head drops, "No, not really."

"It's just that... it would be nice – for mom's sake to be able to bring her some good news," Minerva says with as casual a shrug as possible. Jerry looks away and nods.

Minerva reaches out to pluck a piece of lint off of his shirt. As she inspects the offending piece of fluff, she adds absently, "Well, never you mind. You just keep plugging away. Something's bound to change." She stands back and re-assumes her earlier critical stance.

"Pretty soon you won't have to go looking. Opportunity will come banging on your door – bright young man like you." This time she reaches out to ruffle his hair.

"Mr. Roosevelt seems to be setting things in motion that will get everyone back on their feet again. I hear his family was expelled from Spain during the Reconquista. If so, then it would hardly come as a surprise that he would be inclined to assist those who have been... discouraged."

She tugs at her gloves then turns on her heels. "Well, I'm late for lunch." She waves without looking back, "Don't fill up on popcorn, you'll spoil you supper."

J oe stands absently munching the last of his popcorn in the three hundred and twenty foot lobby of the Loew's State Theater. He adjusts his glasses as he takes in the Daugherty mural of <u>The Spirit of Cinema-America</u>. From the blood-red cloak of the Indian chief on the left to the icy hues of Antarctica on the right, the modernist piece with it's striking use of tiles in primary and secondary colors and its repetition of geometric shapes was like the frozen frame of a kaleidoscope. Joe removes his glasses and huffs breath on his them. He slowly swirls his shirttail with his thumbs on both lenses.

"Can one ever have enough Myrna Loy?", Jerry muses as he sidles up next to his partner.

Joe slips his glasses back on, and slouches his hands into his pockets, "Well, we know Dillinger has." They both chuckle. They stroll out, squinting into the late afternoon sun. Jerry stops and scans the marquees of the other local theaters for likely ways to while away another afternoon.

Joe nods back at the Italian Renaissance inspired lobby doors, "Things haven't been looking so swell lately for lots of gangsters this year, Parker and Barrow, that newsreel we saw... So, those were some racketeer's bodies they found up by Jackass Hill."

"And the film today, if such a thing is to be believed. Not exactly a happy ending."

"Praise be, we now have the Hays office as if people might start thinking crime does pay," Joe said. "Certainly the casting made it look awful glamorous. I doubt that all hoodlums are as noble as Blackie."

"Don't I know it...", Jerry said softly as he starts to move slowly away. Joe let that hang fire and cursed himself silently for for not making the connection between criminal violence and Jerry's family. Jerry and he weren't just friends, they were each others only friends.

Joe shuffles about in his mind for a more engaging subject as he falls in next to his partner, "Something occurred to me while looking at that mural for what must be the one-hundred and eleventh time. You know, how Gould has Tracy in that big yellow coat, and then the fedora and the whole schmeer? It's just so elementary. Not only the color, but the shapes. Striking, simple. We want something that not only catches the eye, but lingers in the mind."

Joe risks a glance at Jerry who strides on seemingly preoccupied. Still feeling the need for a distraction, Joe attempts broaching another tried and true subject, "I've been trying to figure out how I feel about a straight movie bill and phasing out the vaudville. So many great performers began there, Bert Lahr, Jolson, Fields, Keaton, Marx Brothers. And know a lot of their genius is going to be preserved probably for all time, by the very same medium that makes them obsolete..." Now he was starting to depress himself.

"Well, I guess it was inevitable. Like the printing press, movies make ideas and stories available to so many who would otherwise never have had the pleasure of miracles like <u>City Lights</u> and <u>King Kong</u>. Anyway, I think it's definitely got to be *the* art form of the twentieth century." Silence. Then something about the subject of cinema tickled the embers in the back of his mind.

"Oh, hey." Joe purposefully stops, hoping the change of rhythm would help to derail Jerry's thoughts. With a puckish smile he pulls out some new tobacco cards and parts them out slowly for effect: a Carreras oval of Clark Gable; a gleaming grin over his shoulder at the camera. An Ardath card with Loretta Young's yielding moue framed by a rakish fedora brim. Doug Fairbanks, squinting out between a pith helmet and a bow tie.

Jerry dispassionately accepts the offering, flipping through them. Then after a brief pause holds out his hand. Joe smiles and producers the rest of the lot: Myrna Loy with a haughty gaze above her decolletage. Freddy March glowering under a peaked military cap. Merle Oberon looking as glacial as the pearls she toys with at her throat. Carole Lombard with a libidinous simper, looking quite continental in scarf and beret. Doug Fairbanks, Jr. directing his pomaded glare off camera left.

Joe squints critically, "I still prefer the old man."

Jerry flips through the batch, "I don't know. Sure, the father had the swash and the buckle, but the kid has good genes. He may come into his own, yet. Just needs the right vehicle."

Joe shrugged, "Maybe. He just seems, comparatively, kind of slight. Maybe he'd make a better villain."

Jerry laughs, "Not if he's as 'slight' as you suggest. He'd might never make a good 'heavy', like a Chaney or Atwill. But, even an Eddie Robinson needs an aide-de-camp."

"He was good in that Korda flick. Showed some range," Joe finally shrugs.

Jerry holds one particular card up to the light, entranced, "Wow. She was in that one last year with Conrad Veidt, right?" Madeleine Carroll, sleek and swept, luminous in a sheer knit sweater.

"Yep. Conrad Veidt, now there's a strong villain for you," Joe says. "Hey, I was thinking. Instead of Jack Holt, what about Taylor?

"Taylor? Kent?"

"Mm, hm."

"Hmm, Taylor, I don't know... Something punchier, I think." Jerry finishes with the cards and hands them back and offers, "Thanks for the ice cream sandwich."

"Glad you enjoyed it – it's the last."

"What?"

Joe shuffles his feet and ducks his head, "Start delivering groceries for old man Schildkraut. Better pay, better hours..." He shrugs.

Jerry, "Better diet."

Joe nods. Silence.

A realization prompts Jerry, "That probably means less time for-"

"-yeah, probably."

"Swell." Jerry deflates and turns as if to start away again when Joe himself experiences another memory flash so sudden that it actually causes him to bring the heel of his hand to his forehead with a smack, "Oh, my-I can't believe I almost didn't –oh, you got to hear this-"

The sudden alteration to a real, unforced enthusiasm catches Jerry's attention fully. His face contorted somewhere between incredulity and amusement, Joe begins, "You remember the Baurmanns, the Shildkraut's near neighbors?"

'The battling Baurmann's, of course", Jerry readily acknowledging one of the more pugilistic domestic situations in the neighborhood.

"Well, Mr. Baurmann went missing a day and half ago-"

"-His wife's a bruiser, no surprise he'd finally go on the lam."

Joe shakes his head, steps in closer, "The wife said they were sleeping on the fire escape for the heat and you know, their place is three stories up-"

"-yeah-"

"-so, she said he was drinking as usual and took to threatening her with the empty bottle."

"She's disarmed him before."

"Well, this time he follows through and while she's down, her head split, he starts to throttle her-"

"-she says," Jerry says, keeping to the windy side of the law.

"She says", Joe concurs. "Now comes the fabulous part: as he's got her bent over the railing, she's kinda lookin' down, see?" He flexes at the waist in pantomime. "Now, get this-she sees – she sees this guy, running *up* the side of the building. And before she can figure out which one of them is right side up or what, suddenly her husband's not choking her anymore" He straightens up and beams at Jerry's bug-eyes stare,

"What-?"

Joe waves his hands; there's even more, "Not only has his hand been removed, his whole person has been dragged up onto the roof and outta sight."

Jerry tries to to picture this but the mental image keeps rolling around in his mind. To anchor it he stutters out a question, "Wh-what did this guy look like.?"

Joe chortles, "Ah, and it just gets better – she says-get this: he looked like he was dressed for the opera."

Jerry stands there blinking. Something starts to coalesce in his mind about a flapping object, but then an important question sparks from his brain to his lips, "Anybody else see this?"

Joe shakes his head, "Apparently not, but if I were the Shildkrauts, I wouldn't count any too much in the way of character witnesses either."

"So, they're looking for a body?"

Joe shrugs, "If I was the local constabulary I'd start with Kingsbury Run. It's been real popular of late."

"And this is the excuse she gave for her husband going missing?", Jerry spreads his hands inquiringly. Joe shrugs.

"I'd put her on the payroll, if we had one," Jerry says as he turns and collides with another pedestrian. A habit familiar to him from his near incessant reading, he reflexively looks up to apologize when before he can move his lips he hears:

"Siegel, Siegel, birds of an eagle. You guys are just too predictable." He looks up to see to see Glenville High school classmates, Aaron Cohen, and Ruth Karpinsky. Ruth, now a peroxide blonde, very Jean Harlow. Aaron, heat rumpled; his double breasted suit jacket slung over his shoulder, necktie askew, weaves on his feet slightly as he regards the pair.

"What was that about Kingsbury?" He rubs his lower lip in sudden inspiration, "You know...I should suggest to my dad that the bank just buy up the area and find some enterprising, civic minded entity to raze the dump and put something attractive there."

Ruth tugs at his sleeve, "And what about the people who live there?" Aaron stares at her blankly. Joe and Jerry feeling grateful to her for broaching a subject they themselves didn't feel they had the courage to voice.

"Oh yeah... the poor dregs of humanity," Aaron sneered. "Well, once Comrade Roosevelt hands them all a shovel and enslaves them under the government yoke, their future will be secured won't it? Hey, and maybe then they'll be able to afford a loan from our bank to buy the houses we put up. And then everybody will be happy. Is this a great country, or what?"

He beams at them and leans in slightly, "Well, somebody already started the process. You know those bodies they found? My old man says those mobsters must've been killed somewhere else cause there was no blood at the scene. Apparently not even in their bodies. Brings all kinda gruesome thoughts to mind, don't it?"

Ruth tugs even harder at him, "Is that information you should be giving out? You said your father got that information in private conversation."

Aaron yanks his sleeve back, "It's not like these two will do or say anything about it. Their realm is fantasy."

He turns with a smirk, "What about it boys? Fodder for the funnies? What-what is it you two really expect from your little daydreams? I mean, what actual good – what actual *use* are they to anyone? By the way, did you two ever actually graduate?" He turns and giggles at Ruth who flushes uncomfortably.

"Oh, wait, that's right. I heard at least one of you got something approximating a real job. He turns back and squints pointedly at Jerry, "Or any job." But, hey you're the baby of the family, right? So nothing is really expected of you."

Ruth says, "This is the last time you crash one of your father's three martini lunches," as she hooks her arm in his in an attempt to drag him away. But he stands his ground. "Now, now. Not before I wise these rubes up. You boys had better decide soon if you want to stay in the world of fairy tales or commit to doing something concrete in the real world. Because this country is passing the rest of the world by. Let Herr Schicklegruber rant about his master race in the Old World. The real man of tomorrow is here. In the New World. Today. On this soil. He's an American. Or ought to be."

He breaks away and slowly twirls, his head tilted back, "Have you noticed? The skyline of every city is changing across America. We make our own landscape. That's power. The sky is no longer the limit. That's because we got steel. U.S. Steel and I don't mean just for skyscrapers, I mean in the people."

He turns to jab a finger at Jerry, "This country is going places this world has never seen before. You won't recognize it in ten, hell, five years from now. So, don't be a shmo and grab some long coattails if you don't wanna be left behind." The finger comes in contact with Jerry who reflexively looks down as Aaron brings his finger up. Jerry grabs at his stinging nose as Aaron turns and starts off down the street chuckling. Ruth hangs back. Her head bowed, she casts her glance everywhere except at the two, "Umm... sorry, he's – you know, he's-"

Aaron whistles shrilly, then:" Ruth, c'mon, we don't want to be seen with these mustard plasters. People will start to think we got something contagious." Ruth sighs, grits her teeth and stalks after him. When she is level with him she wallops him hard on the arm with her purse and keeps walking. He follows, bleating," Hey, that's the reward I get for my little pep talk...?" And they are out of earshot.

They watch the retreating couple for a few seconds until Jerry's observation,"Ruth looks nice, what with the new hairdo."

Joe," I prefer brunettes."

Another few seconds pass. Jerry finally offers, "Let's call it a day. There's some stuff I need to attend to. I'll call you... soon." Without taking his eyes off of the receding pair he starts off down the street. Joe frowns but keeps still. He calls after Jerry, but not too loudly, "Don't forget the ad in 'Science Wonder Stories for next month's issue!" But Jerry's mind is out of earshot by now.

Almost four hours later, Jerry laces his fingers and extends his arms back and above his head. He groans loudly as his joints pop with the accumulated tension. He settles back in his chair and scans the now tidy desk top with no small measure of satisfaction. Everything neatly filed away, correspondence ready for tomorrow's post; his father would have said it was toygn.

Just one more thing to address. Drumming his fingers absently, he contemplates the envelope from National Allied Publications. An idea floats to the surface of his consciousness from the mental recess he has relegated it to. He rises from the desk and ambles to the phone.

A few minutes later, the mercury still reading almost ninety degrees and nursing an iced tea against his forehead he speaks softly into the phone, "Hey, something occurred to me about our chance meeting with our old school chums earlier."

"Oh hey, don't let that shmok get to you. He's just-"

"-Oh, no. Forget that, I don't care what he says about me its more like... It made me more aware of how much injustice there is in this world and just because it might not occur at the end of gun, that doesn't make the crime any less heinous. In fact it makes things even more insidious."

As he sighs and swigs his drink, Joe responds," It's part of the human condition, I guess. But, it's not like we can ascribe omnipotence as an ability to our character-"

"-No. No...," Jerry replies distractedly. "but, maybe he can be in at least two places at once..."

"What do you mean?", Joe asks.

"I don't know... yet, "He rolls the glass against his flushed cheek and turns his gaze out of the window to the sweltering dark.

Outside the Cleveland Jewish Center, Joe hustles up the entrance steps, "Sorry. I'm late, I know. Old man Shildkraut always seems to find some widow at the end of each day that needs that one last thing they forgot to pick up at the market." He finds Jerry slumped against one of the Doric columns, head bowed over <u>A Princess of Mars</u>.

Jerry snaps his book shut and looks up smiling, "Feel like talking shop? Zorro, not Robin Hood."

"What?", Joe blurts out caught by the seeming non sequitur.

Expansive, Jerry moves about the colonnade, "I was thinking about our difference of opinion on Fairbanks films when out of left field it suddenly occurred to me how Don Diego uses both his own persona and Zorro's to effect justice. How the dual identity protects from reprisals and also allows him access to information he needs for his campaign. And how in contrasting the dual personalities it deflects suspicion each from the other and sort of ...allows him to be in two places at once."

Joe nods, catching up: "No matter what persona he inhabits at any one time, the other will always exist elsewhere in everyone elses mind"

"That also brought me around to the issue of his abilities and how they could isolate him from the very society he is supposed to be protecting," Jerry says. "And more than just for the sake of safety and the need for knowledge, an alter ego would be necessary."

"The 'schlemiel act' not only as a deception, but as a way to keep in touch with his humanity," Joe muses aloud. "So, he's not like a Savage or a Munro, whose aspect is singular, never changing..."

"Funny you should mention 'humanity'. There's something else he could be that they're not," Jerry's smile takes on a mischievous tilt.

Joe's eyes narrow behind his lenses, straining to outguess his partner, "Well... not the occult, we've done that..."

Jerry's face takes on a more sedate bearing as does his pacing, "You're right about that. I think we started this whole idea from the wrong end of the telescope."

Joe cocks his head as if asking for clarification. His partner obliges with alacrity, "Our original idea was a one trick pony and based on a character as dangerous as the despot in Berlin. How does one reach a mind as diseased as Hitler's? If the character is going to have the appeal we're looking for then he has to represent the aspirations that people want to invest in for their future. An aggressive, negative character may not be appropriate now. Certainly not a mindless, soulless Golem wreaking havoc just for the sake of vengeance or some other equally cabalistic individual that's too weird to be widely popular."

Now it's Joe's turn to prop up a pillar as he allows his partner to have the floor. Jerry continues, "Evil is becoming all too real on a global scale. I think our work should reflect that. Because I know that what we do *can* have an effect on people. It's as much about ideas and hope as it is about escapism. To oppose a world view as malignant as Hitler's and a war machine as vast as Nazi Germany is accumulating, there needs to be an equally powerful force."

Joe scratches his head, "Well, strictly from an abilities point of view he would have to be impervious to gas, bullets. Out run a tank. Heck, he'd have to be able to take on a tank."

"A whole division", chimes in Jerry. "But as enormous as these problems are, adversity is planet wide. Here we have epic dust storms and gangsters roiling the middle of the country, overseas the fascist shadow is enveloping more than just Germany, the Japanese are in Manchuria...." Jerry stops his pacing and stops directly in front of Joe, "Allow imagination to ask yourself a larger question: are these problems unique to this planet?" He shrugs," We don't know. But, maybe someone from the outside would have a better perspective."

Joe removes his glasses and massages his forehead as he attempts to reel in the skeins of ideas that have been just been flung at him," ... An... advanced alien... with a dual identity..."

Jerry steps in closer, his voice an insistent whisper with the inspiration of his concepts, "And maybe... he's the last of his race. So, not only does he want to assimilate, he *needs to* in order to have a home. And where better to to learn about the inhabitants of his new home than the land 'whose flame is imprisoned lightning, and her name Mother of Exiles.'"

Joe slips his glasses back on as he responds,"'Send these, the homeless, tempest-tossed to me,'" he nods. "Since he's more advanced, we can assume he'd be rather adept at assimilation..."

"But, the truly powerful thing would be that he does it not just because he has to," Jerry says, "But, because he ends up *here*; a culture that's relatively new, powerful and one built on the premise of justice and equality. Maybe he not only finds these ideals useful, but desirable. It gives him purpose."

Joe smiles and nods eagerly. He checks his watch and grabs Jerry by the elbow and steers him towards the stairs, "And because I'm late, you'll need to walk and talk. It's Jean's turn to cook tonight she'll not be waiting on dinner for anyone." Jerry stares at him nonplussed as they start to move," Where was I?"

"Purpose," Joe offers as he releases his partner's elbow to negotiate the steps.

"Purpose," Jerry smacks his hands together. "Think of it, an Angel of Justice. A Michael, a Gabriel... an Azrael-a voice of God..."

"-Careful," Joe admonishes as he stops and points up and behind them. Jerry follows his gaze. The opaque light of dusk almost renders the words inscribed on the building's pediment obscure, but after a moment Jerry can make out: <u>"Give unto God, the glory due to God's name, Bow down in worship to God in holy beauty."</u>

Joe stuffs his hands into his pockets, nods once more at the building and saunters off, "You don't wanna tempt the lightning." Jerry shrugs his acquiescence and follows, "OK. A... Samson, then to chasten the Philistines."

Fifteen minute later as Joe hops up to the porch he pulls out his keys to let himself in, "We weren't expecting company for supper, so-" Jerry waves him off, "Please, it's OK." Joe steps inside, but leaves the door ajar, "Wait here for a sec..." and he disappears inside.

Jerry turns and toes at the porch railing. He feels there's something important that he forgot to convey earlier. Just before he hears Joe return to the door, it comes to him and he starts speaking as Joe steps outside," I almost forgot. About the alter ego: we need to come up with a profession. Some place large where he can not only blend in, but hopefully can also be an asset in his pursuit of justice..." He stops when he sees:

Joe holding out a starchy, curved sheet of paper, "I know we want to stay away from the previous design, so I just concentrated on the physique." As the sketch only sports a vague outline for the head and facial features, Jerry scans the illustration noting the 'trunks over tights' signature outfit of the muscle man, the stylized cut-away footwear, the shield begging for a revered insignia.

Joe points at the drawing, "I haven't solidified a scheme yet, but I think we should make him as colorful and as distinctive as we can." Jerry slowly fingers the picture as he searches for any comment,"You haven't run out of that wallpaper, yet I see."

"No. no...", Joe says softly after a slightly too long pause. He reaches out and grasps a corner of the drawing and gently pulls it from his partner's grip. "Well...", he turns to head back inside. Just before he closes the door, "Hey, good work today. It's... a lot to digest, but..., yeah..." Just before he disappears, Jerry yelps out, "I call later...!" Joe nods, smiles and closes the door.

Jerry stands facing the closed door and allows a small groan to escape. He knows he should've been more positive in his response to Joe's effort, but after the exhileration of revealing his latest brainstorm, he couldn't muster up the enthusiasm for something that didn't spark an immediate resonance in his breast.

Jerry sighed and stepped off of the porch. The first glimmer of the radiance from ancient spheres begins to pinprick through the deepening twilight sky. On his way home his mind fought a tug of war between guilt and invention until he fell into a seemingly dreamless sleep almost a soon as his head hit the pillow.

For the next few days while the stifling weather made sleeping problematic, Jerry's dreams seemed to amount to little more than a flitting and swooping of images and impressions that left no real residue on his waking mind. So much so that he easily fell into another misanthropic funk. Then one late night, the gates to Morpheus barred by the minefield of his mind, he makes that promised phone call," Didn't wake you, I hope."

Joe clears his throat, "Hm, hmm... no...no... Trouble sleeping?"

"Hm? Oh, no... I don't think so. I just...yeah, I guess that's it...", he sags against the wall, the handset cradled on his shoulder as he toys absently with the cord. "Where you there when people were talking last Sabbath in front of the synagog about how Hitler is also now President as well as Chancellor and what that means..."

"I'm sure for the world it doesn't mean anything good", Joe wipes the sweat from the earpiece and stuffs a tea towel on his shoulder to brace the phone in anticipation of a protracted parley. Jerry suddenly exclaims, "Hey, what about the Babe? Hangin' up the cleats after twenty-one seasons in the big leagues."

Joe leans back in his chair until it creaks, "The deeds of Murderer's Row will live on though they themselves will fade."

"Too bad in a way that some of the most exemplary of us aren't allowed a little more time, more... endurance."

"Noah was given nine hundred and fifty years, how much difference did he make? Does anyone really know?"

Jerry chuckles in response, "I suppose not." Then falls silent. Joe continues to work the creak in the chair as his leg bounces twitchily, shifting his weight to get a different tone. He stops when Jerry's voice comes drifting faintly over the wire: "What do you suppose those who have gone on... or even those who are yet to come have or... will think of us? What we did or didn't do. How we manged to keep the world spinning on into the future? What we have left them to build on?"

Joe realizing that this was the actual thrust of the phone call pauses. He feels a more considered answer would be appropriate, but before he can move on even from that thought, Jerry abruptly stops fiddling with the cord and straightens up and he hears, "Well, I should let you go. You're a working man. While some of us..."

"Jer-"

"Yeah..."

"Our fathers shared more than just a profession and a faith," Joe says quietly. "I think that they each had a great desire to see their children fulfilled and happy."

Jerry replies, "See you soon." And with a small smile replaces the phone in it's cradle and shuffles off to bed.

J erry is standing in his parent's bedroom, watching his father check himself in the mirror on his bureau. He is buttoning the cuffs on one of his good shirts as if he's going out, but it's bright daylight outside. In fact the room is radiant with golden light as if the sun is just outside the window.

There doesn't seem to be any sound but, Mitchell's lips are moving as if he is addressing Jerry without ever taking his eyes from the mirror.

The corners of the room rapidly begin to darken. Gloom presses in from the edges and Jerry feels as if he is underwater. The light is being covered up as if a giant octopus has just inked the room. The pressure, the cold, the thickness closing in until his heart shrinks so small it no longer has any room to beat. And... he's afraid. Truly terrified. He can't see his father. He can't see anything. And now there seems to be a sound that he's not so sure isn't the roaring of the blood in his own ears. He feels like he's being compressed into a ball; a forced regression, jammed into a cold, dark, compacting ...womb. Alone. All alone.

Then... something inside him wells up. It's both a feeling and a word, ...a shout: NO! He feels it in his chest, rising to his throat and he knows it will shatter him if he doesn't let it out so he flings it into the darkness, No! And he stands, fists clenched, arms raised as if he's burst out of a caul of despair. And everything is light. The radiance beams out and dispels all the darkness. The house is gone. His father is gone. Just him in the dazzling sunlight. He lifts his face to the sky and he feels himself rise. Faster and faster, up, up and ...away.

Awake. Suddenly, eyes wide open, staring at the ceiling. Again, he must have dozed off after a hot, fitful night. But, this time he doesn't feel tired. The unconscious has done it's job. Jerry finds images and ideas coalescing. Tumbling one after the other across his mind unbidden. He checks the clock. Almost an hour before dawn. Can't sleep, might as well...

He sits up and rubs his face. Stops. Joe's place is a dozen blocks away and it *is* early. He looks at the clock once more... No. Now. While it still feels inspired. Jerry launches himself from the bed and snatches the envelope from the typewriter and shreds it open with his finger, flips open the single sheet and reads. Three minutes later he is hopping about the room dressing as quickly as he can before slamming out the door without a book in his hands for the first time in weeks.

As he nears St. Clair Avenue, his ears pick up the wail of a distant siren. It seems as if there isn't an hour of the day that isn't tarnished by crime. He slows to a trot to catch his breath when the tortured squeal of rubber cleaves the night air. Two cars whip around the corner. A chattering spray of flame leaps from the lead vehicle. Sparks spatter across the hood of the patrol car in pursuit. It lurches and slides through a picket fence splintering signs that read: 'Blue Flame Gas' and 'Tiolene Oil' and on into a telephone pole. A neon sign at the top proudly displaying 'Chins Chow Mein Served Here' crackles and sparks into fractured darkness. Jerry freezes in the street. The headlamps of the getaway car dazzle his eyes. He raises his hand to shield the glare and starts to fall back to the curb when something large grazes him from behind.

A dark, billowing figure lands in the street twenty feet ahead of him. The figure crouches and leaps again immediately, landing with a clanging wallop on the hood of the escaping vehicle. It wears a dark cape that flows over the windscreen of the car, obscuring all vision from inside. The car heaves from side to side down the street, tires shrieking. Jerry stumbles to the curb as it hurtles by and spins one hundred and eighty degrees to a swaying stop.

The dark, draped body seems to have been flung clear, but it is all happening so fast, Jerry can't be sure. He rocks himself to a sitting position with his elbows. The getaway car is shuddering, it's starter grinding away trying to catch for the engine to turn over.

Jerry looks to the pursuit car. There is no sign of movement. He catches motion out of the corner of his eye. The engine for the getaway car clunks away now under the crumpled hood, the car shuddering into gear. Suddenly, the caped figure lands beside the car and the car engine sputters to a halt.

Muzzle flashes leap from the window, the sound of the shots cracking and singing around the concrete and asphalt as the figure of the mystery man seems to waver and flicker like a candle flame in a draft evading the fusillade. The shooting stops as the car lurches into motion and starts to pull away. As it does, the powerful stranger grabs the rear bumper and leans back. The cars tires are now smoking and squealing with the effort to escape.

More flashes erupt from the car window on the passenger side. The reports barely piercing the tortured sound of the heap straining to escape the steel grip of the stranger. The bumper starts to tear away and the brawny figure then grabs the rear skirt of the car and ducks beneath the under-carriage and seems to disappear for a moment. Then, astonishingly, he appears beneath the car, hoisting it high over his head.

He seems to take a moment to appreciate the panicked reactions from the reprobates of the now elevated sedan. Then with a mighty heave he dumps the car onto the pavement, front wheels first. It comes down, crunching and creaking to a smoking halt. The dust just starts to settle as the titan strides to the wreck and wrenches the diver's door out of the frame. He hauls the groggy driver out from behind the wheel and tosses him to the ground. He stands astride over the prone figure like a colossus.

The passenger door creaks open and the other hood leans over the roof and shakily squeezes off a couple of rounds. They appear to strike the tall stranger in the back. After a moment he impassively turns and fixes his gaze on the gunman. The unnerved thug yelps with fright and turns stagger running away in the opposite direction.

The vigilante watches for moment. Then he casually lopes over to the discarded car door and hurls it like a discus at the fleeing criminal. It catches the crook in the kidneys and in a flash carries him out of sight and into the dark. He then turns and strides menacingly to the driver, who is just now trying to push himself to his feet when he is suddenly hoisted up by the scruff of the neck. Something like a smirk steals across his face as the caped figure holds the crook easily aloft with one hand.

Poised as he is, Jerry can now regard the man's features: a large, broad-shouldered frame, easily over six feet tall. A square face with regular features, cleft chin and blue-black hair that cascades over his forehead. But, it's the eyes which seem to project a red glare over his prey that causes Jerry to suddenly feel as if a line is snapping inside of him. Feeling his energy draining from him through the bottom of his feet, a chilling sweat erupts all over his body. His vision seems to iris out like a silent film transition. He looks down to see the sidewalk seemingly rising to his knees as he crumples to the ground.

This causes the stranger to shift his gaze to Jerry. The man's lips stretch out to a full grin. Something in his smile gleams. Jerry squints to see – just how sharp... and *long*... are they...? Slowly, he turns his back to Jerry and seems to bring his struggling captive closer. Jerry's heart gives a little hop as his eyes roll back and he slowly reclines to the pavement.

A few moments later, Jerry slowly sits up. He woozily observes the cloaked guardian dump the driver's body to the ground. He raises his head almost as if he is scenting the air. Then with a quick glance over his shoulder, the man-hunter leaps to the side of the nearest building with corniced windows. He flexes at the knees then bounds four stories into the air to come fluttering down on top of the granite edifice.

Jerry gapes at this seemingly inconceivable feat, then scrambles up to his feet, alarmed that this paragon of justice might disappear altogether, when – No! He returns to the edge of the corbel edged roof. Arms akimbo, chest thrust out, balancing haughtily like a gargoyle ready to repel any evil. He seems to cast his gaze to the lightening horizon. What do those ruby orbs spy from on high? The future? Duty? Another scofflaw made to face a juggernaut of justice?

The spreading coral pink of the rising sun highlights the red lining of the powerful entity's black cloak. His eyes seem to narrow. Then with a flourish of his cape he turns and leaps out of sight following the darkness. Perhaps to hold it at bay. To roam another night and purge the deepest, darkest shadows of the baser angels of our nature.

Jerry looks around. His breathing coming in astonished gasps. There seems to be some movement at last from the patrol car. Jerry forces his quivering legs to move. Just a stagger at first, but soon he is weaving his way quickly down the street back on his original course.

Twenty minutes later, he stands before a sleep rumpled Joe, gesticulating wildly: "...Crimson or cardinal but... red. Red! Make it emblematic. Like... waving the Stars and Stripes!" Almost as breathless as we was when he first stumbled to the front door, Jerry stands sweaty, mute. His now becalmed hands extended almost as if in supplication. Silence. He becomes acutely aware that the only sounds he can detect in the room are his belabored breathing and hammering heartbeat.

His partners face betrays nothing, his eyes fixed on a point somewhere beyond Jerry's head, "In our sleep, pain which cannot forget falls drop by drop upon the heart until, in our own despair, against our will, comes wisdom the awful grace of God."

Jerry stares at him,"....What?

Joe rises from his chair,"You know the theater can be a wonderful source of education if you pay attention to more than just the backstage gossip."

Then he retreats to his room and momentarily returns with the illustration he had shown Jerry in front of his house. He sits and immediately begins to sketch a few adornments, adding to the drawing with a selection of colored pencils. Minutes later he holds the illustration up and after a brief appraisal, hands it to Jerry. He pushes his glasses up on his nose, settles back in his chair and calmly awaits his partner's reaction.

Jerry takes the sketch and his eyes immediately widen with appreciation. He looks from the paper to his partner and back. The missing piece was like a scroll incarnadine, heralding a champion of rectitude. Head nodding in consent, he delivers his verdict,"Now if we could just submit on something other than wallpaper, that'd be super."

Printed in the United States
By Bookmasters